Earth
@
Stake
State/Craft

Som Nandivada

Solstice Publishing - www.solsticepublishing.com

State/Craft: Earth @ Stake

Som Nandivada

Dedication

To our home system the sun, the third rock, and the rest of the solar family

Curious Indeed

"How about you just stop fiddling with that nostril knob thing for a minute and listen to what I'm saying?" says Joe, squinting angrily.

Man, he is edgy as a hedgehog that's been poked and prodded past tolerance. I don't recollect ever seeing him like this during our prior interactions. From what I remember, he was a fairly calm and peaceful fellow.

Did he really call it nostril knob? Just for that, he is on strike one in my book now.

Besides, I *have* been listening to him. But he just goes on and on, saying the same thing over and over again, so I might as well do some parallel processing while he is at it.

Nobody understands the significance of physiognomy in the context of the work that I do. People don't have the slightest idea as to what it takes, to get a face right.

Sure, on the surface it might seem like I'm just randomly noodling on the tablet, but *this* process is what leads to the final results, to the stuff for which folks like him come to me.

It is the faces that make the narrative, people!

With this strange case that he has brought to my attention now for instance, we're talking about a situation where someone has possibly managed to create the first ever pirate layer that can infiltrate the entire Beacon network and infrastructure, and potentially subvert it. This sounds like a textbook case of a Denial of Service attack.

Now, if so, that *is* a big deal, because Beacon Incorporated is generally considered to be safe from all known forms of attack vectors to date. Their reverse proxies are industry gold standards. This incident, if it really is what it seems, would indeed be a major security breach, potentially of global impact and concern.

It can lead to the opening of the floodgates, and exposure to such future attacks at various corporate networks across the world, all of which are at much lower levels of assurance as compared with Beacon, as far as intrusion prevention goes.

For a matter of this magnitude, heavy duty solutions would be warranted. Accordingly, the rendered faces need to absolutely have the necessary depth and texture. I work off of patterns. When someone describes a person, I see their face in code. That is to say, in my code, like Cuneiform inscriptions coming together.

Per Joe's account, the person in question is by no means a run of the mill personality.

Apparently, he ran into a girl who was dressed in a Beacon outfit. But mysteriously, the beacon misbehaved, and to his misfortune he ended up erroneously concluding that she was beckoning him over, while she was not. He then got ahead of himself with her as he was wont to, and she nearly drew her gun on him. Then right after, she actually did shoot someone else dead, and he was witness to that. Now how can I not start putting a face to *this* narrative right away? Come on!

"This thing is absolutely crazy, Vibe. I was totally losing my mind," Joe continues. "Then I thought of you, and came to you because you've done a lot of them."

"Done a lot of what, exactly?" I ask him.

"Not what, but who; I mean the Beacon crowd," he says, helping himself to a drink. "They are your most cited referral," he elaborates in response to my look of consternation I guess. "You've done more of them than you have from any other corporate entity, so I'm hoping you will be able to help figure this matter out. It is bugging me to no end." He then looks away distractedly at the stained wood fixtures in my cabinetry.

"That sounds morbid, and gross," I tell him. I mean come on, seriously, what is he thinking? "My business is not of a sexual nature, unless maybe laterally so on occasion. And even when so, it is certainly not haphazard or indiscriminate. I don't *do* crowds."

"Sure, man, whatever you say," the fellow grins infuriatingly. "But you have the sharpest tool in the shed for these matters. That much I know."

Yes, people appreciate the results. I *am* proud of my tool, as he calls it. It has given much satisfaction to me, and to society at large.

The Conch, it is an awesome thing.

For those not yet in the know, here's the scoop:

The Conch solves problems, of any kind, in principle. It is based on measure theoretical techniques that are at a higher level of abstraction and generalization than the usual calculus based options, and hence its swath is much broader. Several Conch instances have been deployed that help enterprises sort out their architecture, and provide them with solutions for non-trivial problems.

You can apply a Conch solution to pretty much anything. For example, there are quite a few market analysis oriented conch apps, which are considerably successful from what I hear. Mind you, it is not just for businesses, there is also a prototype implementation which the L.A.P.D. uses that helps them anticipate criminals' moves. The Conch has many such applications, the list keeps growing.

On top of all that, I have this humble hope that in its due time it will contribute to some fundamental science domains as well. For instance, it could help with the study of humans as personality case studies that cogitate, respond to ecosystem stimuli, and in turn affect their environment.

Pharmaceutical companies have already plugged into it. They use Conch solutions to influence behavior, targeted at people who have fed their identities into the applicable conch instances. After all, if properly understood, learning how a person traversed a decision tree in one context can be intelligently applied to tune them biochemically. They can then handle similar future contexts better.

"I really dig Fukitol, man, it is indeed a great success story for you," Joe continues.

Yes, that's another one. I can't help but smile. So, he is a Fukitol consumer, good for him. All right, I'll roll back his strike one.

The Conch app Fukitol determines the measure of the consumer's renunciation level (for whatsoever it is that needs be renounced), when defined thresholds of exasperation are reached. If the required level shows as not yet attained, it tells you how to get there. This targets various non-essential aspects of one's life. It works on the basis of non-pharmacological prescription/subscription based dosages (of 'life coach' type inputs). It helps you to let go of the small stuff basically, by means of helping you to be smart as to when to scuttle it.

In any given situation, there are core problems that do have to be solved. But it is a big challenge to identify that core set and focus on it. Usually we end up squandering precious energy on incidental annoyances that come our way camouflaged and almost inextricably associate themselves with the core problems. It is helpful to figure out how to filter out such incidentals and renounce one's desire to grapple with those. That way we can tackle the core more efficiently. This is what Fukitol helps you achieve.

"Yeah man, just grab that eighth of an ounce of the stuff that counts. As for the rest, Fukitol, and let's get out of the hole," I reply. This tag line is catching on.

Indeed, there are many dimensions to the Conch.

In a Conch take, individual people are represented as actors in use case models, to resort to a cliché. These are very sophisticated models though, highly faithful in terms of representation. The thing to be aware of when thinking in terms of a classical use-case based model as applied to a Conch instance, is that in this context, the actors are *in* the system. They are not just being represented within the system by some icons while themselves being external to it.

It is immersive, in short.

I know, yet another cliché. The term is old and much used, but it keeps acquiring new meanings, and people now associate it with the Conch.

The interactions within a conch take are state-of-the-art VR. That is to say, they're virtually real. The subscribers and consumers of conch instances feel like they are absolutely living the experience which the model renders. They walk out of the sessions and continue to carry the world view from therein, for a good bit.

"Talking of holes ... the one you got us out of back then at Chariot, man that was one hell of an exit ride. Was it three years ago?" muses Joe.

Yes it was; tempus fugit, and so on. I guess it was a reasonably good gig, although I do have mixed feelings about it.

The Chariot trademark service started out as an anti-snore solution, and grew from there. Now they say that it also helps you sleep better in various other ways. It gets feeds from your day's context (your office VPN, your phone, your social profile, etc.). It then plugs into your pillow, and once you lie down, it interprets those feeds, resolves the day's stress points, and improves your sleep. Or so they say. Yeah, right.

Man, that gig was all gas actually. Given all the insomniacs whose number keeps increasing by the minute, what with all the anarchy and chaos out there in the world, sleep is becoming a rather precious commodity these days. Chariot's offering is the same old smoke and mirrors, in a new package. Who can really track whether such products actually do what they promise?

Anyway, at that time, Joe was an actor in the scene for a conch deal I was engaged in, at Chariot.

They were deploying a showcase to demonstrate a chained sequence of perspective shifts that chariot consumers would experience. First there would be the onset of sleep, and then progressive shifts into increasingly pleasant chariot induced states. The conch session was basically to put on a show about how the whole thing works. You could call it a marketing media segment thing.

For this scene, during the action takes, Joe was the guy who laid his head down on the pillow. I remember the quizzical look on his face when just as he was about to do his first take, he had asked me, "What is this thing?"

For a moment, I had not known what to tell him. Come to think of it, what *is* a Conch immersion, exactly?

I further remember scratching my head haphazardly for a bit, looking for insight from within on how to describe it.

"There was this balladeer named Bob Dylan, from a while back," I'd said finally. "He was from before the parameterized post-modern age, born about a Century and three quarters or so ago. Do you know of him?"

"Nope," he'd replied.

What a world … No one seems to know much these days. But still everyone gets by somehow, just skipping along like flat rocks on water, no idea as to what is below the surface.

"Look up his life some time, it will do you good," I had told him. "At the start of his career, Dylan moved from

Minnesota to New York. He then became a bit of a street child there. The way he went through the life there during his early days in NY, and how the gaslight scene played out in his head as he was making his way through it - *that* is pretty much what immersion is, and is how the conch works. You are in it and a part of it, even if you're just passing through. And it stays with you after."

Joe seemed to know what the gaslight concept is. The term broadly signifies the pell-mell life of greasy food joints and entertainers and live shows and the underground music scene, and such likes. He knew all that, so he got the gist of the reference, even if he doesn't know who Dylan is.

Then he immersed like crazy, right from the first take.

In fact, he did so well and the whole presentation was so successful, that consumers were sold even tighter on the Chariot product. On top of that, they wanted to themselves immerse in the associated conch takes.

Talk about riding the gravy train! I was then able to deploy field installations to Chariot so that they could sell immersion sessions as side deal perks along with their core product. Of course, I got my cut which felt pretty decent at that time.

That trip lasted a good long while, but then someone sued for having incurred headaches and frizzy hair or something, allegedly because of the conch apparatus, and all of a sudden, I was a pariah at Chariot. I desperately needed help to dig myself out of the hole, but no one would even throw me a bone.

Finally, the savior was Emmy, my partner in crime for the Conch. She called one day most unexpectedly, while I was down in the dumps. We had drifted apart over time and had not been in active touch for a while, but for this situation she came through, and bailed me out by means of a quick cryptic message.

"Sell them the pain," was her gist.

It took me a while to get her point. But once I did, I started to socialize it across the corridors and aisles of the movers and shakers of Chariot.

To my amazement, the idea *really* took off. Sell them the pain, like literally. People really dig it. There is even a BDSM-as-a-Service variation of this that is doing the rounds I believe.

The uptake was so good that the revenue surges pushed the envelopes of all kinds of exponential models, left and right wherever the uptick could go.

As to myself though, I was quite rotten at inking contract deals back then, so I just stayed at my paltry initial cut terms. But Chariot Inc. skimmed much cream off of this concept.

Yes, to sum it up, the conch duals for the subscribers, as the actors in the conch sessions are denoted, are pretty much as good as their own selves would be, within the given session context at any rate.

This is also why Joe was saying I *do* people. He is right I guess, in some sense.

Anyway, the Conch – it is not just a tool, or even a set of tools. It is a system, a framework, and more. It provides maps and projections from State A to State B, of people and situations combined. It tackles problems, and offers solutions.

But yes, when I operate it from the media room, it does convey the sense of a specific tool set, and I'm OK to go along with that.

Ah, the media room! What a thing of glory it is, my pride and joy. The local argot has denoted it as the *igloo*, due to the shape the guided wave layers have accorded to it. There are so many art forms at play here. Just consider the signal processing and communication systems for instance, the intricacies will make your hair stand on end.

I do like the name, the igloo. It is like a garage for the Conch. It is where the conch instances are born.

When I'm in my igloo, I always think of Emmy and Bonar. The three of us spent so many pioneer moments here together, working as a team and giving life to the Conch.

They both had deep ties to Beacon. He was a vendor of record there, back then when we first built it, and she was a networks and telecom security engineer with them. She is continuing on in that role even up to now as a matter of fact.

That aside, while on their personal clock, they were also the co-founders of the Conch along with me. In fact, Bonar I would say had the largest input into the seed ideas that went into the product.

Yes, he had the visionary design. Emmy ran with the complexities of the build. Mine was the foundational concept.

I already had some digital property that I had developed as a part of my research work from before, a set of measure theory based solutions that ran on spatial data. That old application of mine could predict paths for particles under spatiotemporal constraints, simplistically put. I transferred over a whole bunch of subroutines from there, into this new engine.

So yeah, it was the three of us basically.

Emmy and Bonar are also the reason why I have a much bigger footprint at Beacon Inc. today, than I do anywhere else. They've swung some hefty muscle there, both of them, and that has proven to be a very beneficial legacy for my current Conch based income.

The Beacon is my biggest revenue source.

As a corporation, Beacon Inc.'s mainstay is a biometrics based dating system called the beacon. The beacon merges geo-location tracking features of some of its predecessor online dating apps with its patented biometrics technology that identifies and tracks human arousal states. It can inform subscribers when a potential match or someone they are interested in was turned on by them or not.

Joe is an archetypical Beacon client. He swings and rolls with the machine. He is a premium user, from what he tells me, although he also says that he is thinking of steering off of it now, there is something about it that no longer works for him. Possibly this incident has jolted him, and that could be the reason.

Coming back to the incident itself, to summarize, he got a beacon signal lock with a girl but something misfired and things went haywire at personal interaction level.

"So, what is the core problem here?" I ask rhetorically, but I guess my scowl drives him to respond.

"Well, why did the beacon glitch?" he asks. I nod at him, feeling somewhat bemused. I get it, but what does that mean though, exactly?

A beacon is basically a bunch of smart apps, built on a cloud based software-as-a-service solution for extreme, real-time dating, with the physical reactions of the subscribers concurrently reflected in the system to optimize the success rate, all tied in with branded clothing. The standard setup comes with a flagship jacket that holds the main smarts. There are a host of other configurable offerings as well.

Joe says he never bought into the jacket idea, since it did not work for his aesthetic. So he invested into the configurable wardrobe items more extensively. Well, there are different ways to skin the cat as they say. That is one strange expression though, not sure which human culture has the palate for cat meat, but I digress.

Coming back to the point, a functional beacon ensemble uses IPv6 based intelligent wardrobe and wearable accessories, with some heavy duty built-in geo-tagging functionality. When there are 2^{128} addresses to choose from, you can basically program what you wear, in virtually unlimited ways. The machine can get into all your nooks and crannies. Beacon Inc. has tapped into this address pool in a very smart fashion. The system can sense whether the person is turned on, and acts as an arousal beacon that will convey to a nearby potential rendezvous partner (who also needs to be a subscriber of the beacon services of course), that the odds are good. It basically cuts to the chase by increasing the chances of getting lucky.

Of course, as we should know by now but invariably forget every time, there is no such thing as a free lunch. In this case, the cut is not just to the chase, it also shaves off a good chunk of the thrill. Although Beacon does aver that they are capable of compensating whatever is lost with an equal measure of thrill and/or pleasure, but that is open to interpretation.

That aside, when you partake of this kind of stuff, you become a form of processed meat yourself. Me, I'm not canned goods, no way. It has always been just a select few folks that I have managed to even get along with, let alone considerations of going any further, except for pure-play physical for which I don't really see the need for a technological aid. At a deeper level, I've only had one sustained relationship, and that was quite a while ago.

I can never see myself as a beacon subscriber.

Anyhow, let's get back to the problem on hand.

Technical malfunctioning is always possible. Granted that Beacon is a paragon of service excellence and they meet very high standard non-functional requirements, but in principle, a malfunction can always occur. What we need to ascertain is as to whether there was any hue and cry at Beacon at all for this occurrence, whether there was an incident that was caught and noted, or not. The help desks have no information according to Joe, so it is not looking like a technical glitch for a real beacon customer, which that girl might not have been, in any case. Quite likely the ensemble was stolen, in which case one would expect some trace of it. Considering the price and sensitivity of the merchandise, at a minimum a physical inventory discrepancy or a missing pick/pack/ship transaction ought to have been logged in the system, one would think?

If not, then it indicates a more intelligent subversion, and someone has a willful and possibly malevolent interest in breaching Beacon's perimeter, for whatever reason.

This is what we really need to dig into.

So, what can the Conch do to solve this? From what he tells me, the glitch girl is gone, the one he was hitting on. She has walked her way out into the sunset, along with her beacon outfit. Can we now even solve this, without finding her? Or as a first level goal, do we necessarily have to get a hold of her? Can we even think of doing that? She is dangerous as per Joe's narration, and we are civilians unskilled in dealing with such street matters.

It probably does make sense to use the Conch to support this decision and determine next steps. I can see why Joe has come to me.

Per intended design, the Conch is meant to execute path integral algorithms, similar in concept to my simplistic path predictors which I'd built a while back for models in dynamical systems. The Conch objective is to use measure theoretical methods in deep learning, to find operator algebra based solutions for defined problems, based on operators that take a context and crunch it to find *good* path integrals. Taking from all this, it renders annotations on occurring reality that help the subscriber choose the best possible option for any situation.

This basic deal has evolved from concept to prototype, all the way until now where it is a fully operational service offering for enterprises, states (i.e. governments), and other miscellaneous social consumers.

I now have a service portfolio and a well-published catalog, where I offer context crunches.

People keep knocking at my door for this.

This Joe guy today for instance, he is not just window shopping. I believe he does mean to hire me to do a Conch take on this matter of his. As soon as he does though, he is going to want a sneak preview at the igloo. I remember his giddy excitement during those Conch renderings of the chariot scenarios. Yes, it was about three years or so ago I think it was, as he said.

He works as a product beta tester there at Chariot. And before that, I believe he used to be a sales guy at Beacon for a while.

Yeah, for this thing he will want to hit the igloo, for sure.

For tonight though … shoo, fella. I got things to do.

Damn, but he just won't wind down, will he? Well, let me take in the source feeds from his narrations, and then I'll kick him out soon as politely possible.

Not that he is going to go back all the way to L.A.

Nope, he will hang out somewhere closer, probably on the Pacific Coast along the Highway, and keep bugging me till he gets his sneak preview.

"Man that was crazy! I've never heard of a beacon that misbehaves, it is a humdinger I tell you. On top of that, it happened with someone as sexy as that, and as vicious as hell. I know the street, man, and I can survive any situation. But she was something else," Joe says. He has been saying pretty much this same thing for the past half hour already.

It is true though, what he is saying, it *is* a humdinger. Beacon Inc. has gone to crazy lengths to ensure that their products and services are failsafe. That is why they are so expensive.

"I contracted out for top of the line port sniffers to figure out some location intelligence, but so far nada, zilch, nothing …, I've no idea where the ensemble for which I got the signal lock with is from, and no idea where it might now be," he says.

"Did you raise it with the digital supply chain helpdesk @ Beacon? I know it is a pain to stay on the line with them but they might be able to throw some light on it?" I ask.

He grimaces and nods.

"Of course, buddy. I'm persistent, I'm obsessed, and I've been on it like a hound dog," he responds, "but struck nothing as yet, just keep chasing mirages along the help desk transfers of line. It is really bugging me, starting to feel like as though I'm at a ball game that is dragging out to the nineteenth inning or something, and I just can't leave till the game is over."

"Well, I have a couple of questions," I interject. "Firstly, how does it help to employ smellers of fortified wine for this goal? The other question is a deeper one: if the game is dragging that long, there will be grumpy folks around you, kids bawling alongside since the concession stands would have all shut down a while back, and other such irritants, and it really won't be a fun day out any more. So wouldn't it be rather bothersome to stay put till the game is over? It's just a game; why not just bail out in good time?"

"Hey these port sniffers are not what you're thinking of, they are network programs," he clarifies for the first one. I know that, I was just messing with him. The guy doesn't get a joke does he, notwithstanding his name.

What a handle he has got huh, last name Kerr, given name Joe.

Well, the joke is on his detractors though, because he is a hot shot, and is in the inner circles with the bros in the hoods around Hollywood. He is bloody rich, so to speak.

That's why he can afford to commission gigs like this on personal whims. Not that I make much off these deals, but the pass-through costs for setting up the right media elements, and the infrastructure and bandwidth etc. for the takes, that kind of stuff all adds up significantly.

There are many cogs and many wheels in this machine, and many gears, rotors, motors. You name it, the machine has it. To make all of that work together, at pretty much every level, you have to deal with mom-and-pop vendors, and say uncle every now and then. I just hold the keystone element for the Conch, but there are so many others who have their grip on various other pieces. The rest of it adds up quite a bit, and then it all can get to be rather heavy on your wallet. What can you do, man? It's the machine. You just keep feeding the beast.

In a way, it is good that he has done some investigative leg work already but is nonetheless clueless as yet. The odds of the case being a bummer are reduced to at least that extent, and I can hope for a more interesting gig.

"Secondly," he continues, "bawling kids or not, to continue using your analogy, I just *have* to see it out till the end, I don't walk out of the game. That's just who I am."

Okay, then.

"So, during the cited occurrence, when you got a match on the beacon, was it for a named user?" I ask, although I don't expect that to be the case. Sure enough, he shakes his head, indicating negative.

"That was why the Beacon customer service desk and the other departments I reached into, none of them shared any of the real detail, however hard I tried," he says.

Only the lowest rung, the cheapest tier of subscribers, will be named users, and the authentication protocols lay them bare, pretty much, and anyone can track them down. Premium levels allow for various degrees of identity masking and protection, and for premium customers the identity gradually resolves only for the private perusal of the beacon match, once acknowledged.

So the girl Joe ran into remains nameless, at least for now. Although she did mention a given name rather quirkily, in the narrative he is spinning. It doesn't jive though, since he said she is Latino and Heidi is typically a European name. She might be using it as a code name of course.

It is an intriguing case, for sure.

Joe asks for some snacks, and looks askance at the bag of peanuts I proffer. The nuts come bagged in his name too, at that. It's Trader Joe's.

What is he expecting? I don't stash beluga caviar in my stock.

Appearances can be deceptive. Yes, the woodwork is fancy in this bungalow but it's not mine. I'm just renting this place. The guy who owns it seems to have a soft spot for UCSC floater populations, e.g. post docs like me. That is why the rent is cheap for something this swank.

The owner doesn't know though, that I'm an academic only on the side, and I have a more tangible revenue stream via the Conch. Otherwise, I would have been stiffed with a much higher rent I'm sure.

It's not that much of a stream though, as yet. I just get by, which is kind of why I've continued as an academia side floater for quite a while now. Riding two horses concurrently, what can I say?

Some people call me Paapad. It is the name of an Indian appetizer snack, but in my context it stands for the guy who continually stays put, out at the fringes of academia, the Perennial Post Doc, or PPD, hence Paapad.

My given name is Vibhuti Bhushan. People mostly know me as Vibe.

Also, on account of what appears to be some genetic form of cool headedness in my demeanor, some people also call me the Sanguine Man, a stretch drawn from my last name Sangma. Yeah, I *am* cool, why should I soft pedal it. My ancestry is from Shillong after all, in India. I belong to the Garo Hills, where we're all cool cats.

Anyway, regarding this case - here is what has happened with Joe, the said incident that he is not able to shake off, which has brought him to me seeking Conch services.

He came across an attractive woman at a strip mall in an L.A. suburb. With utmost delight, he saw that he had scored a lock-in on a beacon match, and so he made his move. To his consternation, she wasn't having any. Instead, she almost cut his balls off, so to speak.

In a state of frozen panic, he noticed a further twist to this horror story he had walked into. There was a lurking thug at the other end of that sidewalk strip, who was about to take a shot at her. So, in a reflex, Joe warned her.

The woman then calmly took out her own firearm, and plugged the thug one right in the center of his forehead between his eyeballs.

Then, as a measure of gratitude, considering that Joe had saved her life after all, she gave him a tip that he could cash in on, at any one of those shampoo dunk joints that a lot of people are fascinated with these days but only some actually go to. And then she walked away.

That is basically what happened, in a nutshell.

This was a few weeks ago.

And now, even as of today, he is still terrified at times, on account of the initial scare and shock that he got when she had turned out to be not only *not* a romantic match, but to further rub salt on his wound, was actually a fearsome and threatening jezebel.

This spooked state of his is partly the reason why he is guzzling on my alcohol stock so much, I guess.

I'm surprised though, because I know from his background that he is a tough enough guy. He is often out and about on the streets of L.A. for goodness sake, and that is no small feat these days! This girl must have been something else indeed, to have scared him so.

He has reason to be afraid no doubt, but is nonetheless unable to shake off the fact that a glitch occurred with a beacon.

I do see where he is coming from. Beacon Inc. is a veritable paragon of secure infrastructure and failsafe functionality. It *is* a strange occurrence indeed. To either of our knowledge, this kind of a thing has never happened before with Beacon.

So now, he is so much worked up about it that he wants to commission me to look into it.

I'm revved up for it too. It's a damn good case. But the fellow is rather pushy and that can get annoying.

"Yeah, so when can you show me the first cut?" he asks, like right on cue.

"You're presuming quite a few things here, buddy," I parry.

I carve out my own time, always. It's a first principle. It is crucial for me to retain the leverage on this front in the gigs that I take on. It's the only way I can load-balance.

"Fair enough, my friend," he grins. "You see, I'm from Compton, straight out of, pretty much. I got attitude, and, when I want something, I've got to have it."

"You are not from there, not really," I counter. He lives in Manhattan Beach.

He is of mixed origins: Afro-Caribbean and European roots. His base complexion is an unusual shade of burgundy, with occasional tinges of ruddy at certain angles. He has a seasoned and weather beaten look.

All said though, he's from the hood all right. So I know what he means.

Just look at how he dresses up, all-white suit with a black-and-white polka dot shirt underneath, snazzy tie thrown in casually and not too tight, black soles on shiny white shoes. Underneath the suit of course he has the same beachcomber look which I know from before, dreadlocks and all, albeit flawlessly and meticulously coiffured and maintained like only a very rich man can afford. He is a sharp dude.

"I may not literally be from that exact neighborhood," he replies, "but you know what I'm saying. I've seen the world, buddy. There has been a phase of life where I've been homeless, situations when I've done time in the storm tunnels under the Las Vegas Strip. I then got sick of the parts of the world which man has messed up, and trekked the Sierra Nevada for months on end, living off the land in the Great Basin watersheds and the deserts. Folks call me Mojave for the time I've spent there; that desert has got the firmest grip on every fiber of my being. All in all, I've grown from the ground up, Vibe."

Interesting … Well I can work with him, all in all. He is a decent enough fellow.

But generally speaking, it sucks to be at the beck and call of anybody's hustle. That is why I draft my contracts around well-defined statements of work, with *my* choice of weasel words.

"Why don't we pick it back up, come Wednesday around daybreak?" I suggest.

But he wants to firm it up *now*. Well he is paying, so okay, customer is king, and we *have* to make the deal now. Sheesh, where's the breathing room these days?

Well the good thing is, with Joe, I do have history from back when I'd done gigs at Chariot Inc., so we have common language, and it is fairly easy to draft the agreement and the statement of work.

He of course continues to hit my drinks cabinet quite liberally while we are in the process, making it an even simpler matter to put the ink on the paper.

I'm quite keen on this one.

Soon as Joe's gone, I am going to initialize the Conch session for this occurrence.

But he doesn't go easy now, does he? Nope, he can talk, and talk, and talk.

Eventually we do crawl our way out to the exit; yes, it's time to wind down, thankfully.

Still, he takes his sweet time to suit back up, and horn in his shoes, and finally …

I see him out the door, and shortly thereafter, to clear my head I step out myself to take a short stroll round the bend, just enough to have a view of the ocean through the redwoods. That makes my day, any time.

Santa Cruz is an amazing place. Usually, towns named for male saints have the prefix 'San' and those named for female saints are prefixed by 'Santa'.

So the cross is considered female then, for having borne Jesus Christ during the crucifixion. Or so this town believes.

It's a surfer town, just south of the core of Silicon Valley. Once upon a time, it was a hub for the manufacture of gunpowder for the mining industry. The Physics department here at UCSC, with the heritage of the Dynamical Systems Collective, all in all it is an awesome place to be in. Yes I like it here.

Indeed, Santa Cruz does stand apart.

Conch Take – The First Draft

It's a breezy and pleasantly chill afternoon. Rambling away the day on the boardwalk at the pier, is pure bliss.

A nice, bright looking girl rides by on her bicycle waving at me in passing, makes me happy. Man, the California air is so good I could just disperse myself into it. Yes that'd do it for me, don't need much else.

But that's not all there is to existence, is it? Nope, there's the routine muck to deal with.

I've got stuff to do, and deliverables that are due. I should get going.

Still, I procrastinate as much as possible.

It is nice outdoors and I'd rather kick around and just loaf here, but that's not the only reason. I'm dragging my heels also because of a prescience of dread, which I've managed to somewhat suppress so far by focusing on the pleasant surroundings.

I don't know what to make of it. I've started to feel this way a lot these days. It's in keeping I guess with the increase in the level of anarchy we are seeing all around, the world order falling apart bit by bit. Santa Cruz at least is still a bit of a haven in that regard.

Anyway, I just dawdle and hang about town randomly for a while longer.

Fukitol doesn't cut it for me anymore; I know the core logic too well. I'm pretty much on my own as far as handling my demons is concerned.

As the twilight hour arrives, my head gets even gloomier. A sense engulfs me that there is some strange, ominous darkness lurking just at the edge of the town. Not

Santa Cruz in a literal way, but the greater town, the world, existence, everything.

Ah, let's just shelve the heebie-jeebies and get on with the day.

Heading back inside, up the short set of stairs leading to the porch and into the house, I'm upbeat again. I imbibe and infuse as customary from the celebratory offerings of the moment till due satiation is achieved.

It is now time to get on with the business on hand, got to get going with the Conch.

Whatever jitters I've got for this specific gig, working with the tools of the trade is always a pleasure.

What can I say about the Conch, for the benefit of those not yet versed with it?

At the simplest level, it renders occurrences for repeatable immersive participation and review.

The presentation aspect of the service catalog engages the consumer. Under that hood, there is a decision support layer that provides measured takes on pertinent matters within and for a given occurrence.

The way it works is that you have to keep shoving stuff, like premises and hypotheses, et cetera, at the inference engine. Again, it's the same precept; you've got to feed the beast. That is how the duals mature, and their personality develops.

From that you get *measures*, which are your takeaways to be used as deemed fit for the contexts and situations you fed into the conch, from this supposedly real world.

"Yo Doc, what's up?" says Bootstrap chirpily.

Damn, it is really getting to me, this persona thing of the startup sequence. But I need Emmy to adjust such settings and change it up a bit. She could do it remote too, but she's not had cycles even for that, for quite some time now. Hopefully someday soon she will.

Till then unfortunately, Bootstrap will chug along just as blithely.

Anyway, let's do the first take on Joe's case. It's an oddball, since it is not tied to any corporate objective, but rather is intended to satisfy the curiosity of an individual, to address his personal whim.

This is a new concept for me. My deals hitherto have been with corporations, or with their underbellies in some form or the other, not with a free agent individual. I never had occasion so far to directly deal with anyone *that* loaded. Well, you live and learn every day. For this one, I got the contract, so I'm good, that's all I care about.

Okay, let's crank it up.

There is a lot of machine intelligence in the igloo. It can get scary sometimes. But it is a fantastic invention.

And it's mine!

Of course, I am not an inventor, not by any stretch of the imagination. For the Conch, I had some ideas, and I played a part in the drafting of the rough blueprint. Further, I consolidated the inputs from others and of course added my own, and am now driving the operational end state.

The way the cards landed, the Conch, igloo and all, became my proprietary entity, modulo some adjustments and partnership aspects to be sorted out.

There have been ever so many collaborators along the road that have contributed into its current state. Most of them have moved on, having received their due share of the property. Also, with each new deal, I do keep giving some more back to some of them as service based apportioning, depending on as and how they contribute. It's a demand and supply network after all. I'm not a one man shop.

Of the original core collaborators, Emmy somehow never really settled up properly or worked out her cut in a finalized way.

As to Bonar, he had just completely vanished, long before this setup became operational. He was a Vendor of

Record at Beacon Inc., but no one there that I was able to check with knew where he might be at now. I don't either. There's another mystery for you. I could maybe spin up a conch gig to solve that, but who'll foot the bill!

Man, I'm drifting … let's focus on the job on hand.

The resolution that Joe is looking for from the crunch of this context is, how and why did a beacon generate erratic readings? He is quite obsessive about things like product guarantees and the track record of any item, pertaining to wherever he has a footprint in the consumer goods and services markets.

In this particular case, some further background context is that he has deployed some add-on business services on top of the beacon deal that serve a sort of underground ghetto scene layer. He had set this up back when he was on the sales team for Beacon, and seems to still be skimming off the top from it. So he has some kind of a direct stake in this matter as well, I guess.

I used to wonder as to why he takes on these ball-and-chain jobs with corporations when he is already so well loaded. But I suppose this is how he further grows his money, via such add-on services, which would not be possible unless he has an inside angle.

Regarding this incident, Joe believes that to date this is the one and only known occurrence of this problem. There have been zero forum complaints or any such trace, of any other occurrence of this nature. He is quite positive that this is the first time ever, and he is obsessing on it. I can understand his situation; it is crazy indeed, what he described.

Okay, so what do we have here?

I put the VR headset on, gorilla glass organic LED nested screens and all, fully stereoscopic sensory inputs. The sweet juices of the other world start to form.

"Have a good trip, Doc," says the annoying Bootstrap, going quiescent finally.

The visor has the metadata pointers for and connectivity with the other active media elements in the room, that all feed in into the Conch session, each element routed and guided in per corresponding waveguide form.

The cusp based, conch shaped, modular packaging of the core assembly within the igloo is meant for the waveguide formations. It is all Emmy's engineering brain at work. This shape of the core assembly is the reason for the name, the Conch.

The waves superpose, reflect, refract, and scatter in various permutations and combinations of the signals transmitted from the igloo elements, as also from within the multiple panes of the gorilla glass layers, different polarization parameters in each layer. It is all designed and built for exquisite, multi-dimensional rendering.

It is an awesome contraption, but at the same time, I'm not soft pedaling the challenges at all. For instance, the information exchange in the communication systems between the layers heats up the glass. That can get quite ugly.

So to address that particular problem, we built heat exchanger systems to almost immediately convert the heat into further signal strengths. This way, you win on both sides of the coin. The rendering improves, as also the head gets just nicely toasty, no more, and no less. Goldilocks would approve.

Yeah I could go on about the Conch, but let's stay focused. We have to do the draft of a take today.

Let me pull the locale first. Joe was mentioning that it is just off of Century Boulevard.

Man, that area is the very belly of the beast. He had also mentioned that the building was very much industrial looking, at odds with the surroundings. Ah, there it is, I got it, the Laundromat place.

The commencement of a conch take is usually via situation-based conversation snippets. If the context doesn't have active conversations, then possibly you could feed in some monologues to kick it off.

There are other ways to instantiate sessions too, of course. Not every use of the Conch involves dialog, or even monologue.

Anyway, for this one - as input for the take, here's what I got from Joe's description:

It is a regular day, in a seedy slice of L.A. The scene is right outside a Laundromat in an Inglewood strip mall.

Joe sees a Latino girl at the corner of the strip, in a rough spun, white-hot calico skirt with stockings underneath, sporty top, and a signature Beacon jacket. She's got a sharp oval face, and her skin gleams and glistens in the sun.

She looks at him too, sizing him up, and then turns back and peers into the alleyway at the side of the Laundromat.

The building has a façade that is done up to resemble old style brick and mortar buildings, much like the manufacturing plants of pre-crash Americana. This is in stark contrast to the adjacent edifices, which are all prefabricated and reinforced, based on the various composite materials that are in closer keeping with the mores of the day. Also, perversely, this strip mall is set to some kind of a Byzantine theme of sorts. Overall, it stands out as particularly retro.

Joe sees a beacon lock on the girl's prospects, walks up to her, slides his hand around her waist, fondles her down the side, reaching in between the jacket and the top, saying "hey there, sugar bush," fully expecting to score.

She gazes intently at him, and adjusts her carriage with a multi-level swivel such that his hold slips.

A reverse motor shock from her receding touch hits him in the head, and as he looks into her eyes, he sees that he has been spared and is still alive, only because she is checking him out for the moment.

"I'm sure you've got your cojones in working order. But I have a pair of my own, you know," she responds calmly. "I always carry them with me; they go by the names of Smith and Wesson."

She has got one hand half way into her purse, and the other one is millimeters away from Joe's family jewels.

As if this situation is not surreal enough, out of the corner of his eye Joe sees a professional killer in the alleyway starting to take aim at her, and swears, "what the ...", and pulls her in.

She sees the look of panic on his face, and in a quick reflex, takes her gun out, takes aim from cover, and shoots the other guy dead.

"I should just shoot you down as well, for good measure. *Nobody* gropes me, ever ..., nobody," she says.

"But I will let it go," she continues, "since you helped save my life after all. And don't say I'm not generous. I'll give you a little extra on top. If you're ever at a shampoo dunk, just tell them Heidi sent you," she hands him a card, and walks off down the sidewalk along the alley, casually hopping over the corpse along the way.
<<Pan in, like just so ... and ...>>

There she goes ... and ... she is gone.

Yes, got it, the first draft of the conch take for this gig.

It's on persisted media now, but still a bit wobbly. Good enough for a first take I guess.

Hmm, now I have to crunch this proper. There is more detail in the notes I got from Joe, need to feed it in over further takes, as also continue to receive and process inputs.

Now, should I stay somewhat plugged in myself, or just give it turnkey to my conch dual? Huh ... I'm not sure yet.

My dual did get that fleeting glimpse of Heidi around the bend, so let's see how he mulls on it.

What was that reference Heidi made, the shampoo dunk joint? Hmm, let me look it up.

Ah, this is the kind of service that you find in the certain salons where you would lay down your head and the salon staff would do their thing. Yes, I have seen them around these joints. I don't know the inside scoop but I'm pretty sure it's not just your head that comes into the mix. I have a hazy recollection of a bootleg ad of theirs, 'we're hard on your head, but gentle on your genitals.'

Now this is interesting - per the search results (some of which incidentally I'm able to access due to my 'good citizen' standing with law enforcement), it seems that this dunk technology has been intercepted by the drug cartels. Instead of intravenous and up the nose and all such jaded old methods, they have now found new avenues to achieve highs by 'injecting' the shampoo dunk with so-called upgrade packages.

The game is getting exciting! Well of course, if the glitch girl was able to casually kill somebody right on the street and walk on nonchalantly, there has to be a Cartel angle. Such an obvious aspect, duh, I should have anticipated that.

Okay, so logically, the next thing we have to do is get Joe to go there to one of these places, act per his cue, and present Heidi's card. Presumably, that will help see him through the rough patches in that experience. And if we're lucky, will also give us a glimpse of the steamier side of the story.

And then, maybe we will crunch *that* as Session Two of Joe's Blow.

The Conch sessions are stakeholder views basically, and the actual people are represented in context of those views, by their duals. If the real person signs off on the identity fine print, then the rendering can get quite detailed and spot on, in terms of faithful representation of the originating personality. Otherwise, their dual remains as a stick figure shadow, with just generic features.

The duals are personality projections. They are also denoted as 'blow persona', since technically speaking, a consenting participant is having a blow at the conch.

My dual is of course well defined whenever I happen to actively participate in a Conch session, as are the duals for Emmy and Bonar. The three of us had ended up committing our identity deals right at the outset, signed up to all the terms and conditions in their glory.

So, for us, the upside is that any of us can plug into any Conch gig and get our dual to run with the ball, basically.

We are the only globally declared duals in the machine, albeit dormant in any given local instance unless explicitly invoked, like how I did for my dual for this session.

On occasion we have added other people, sure, but we have kept the rights to add and delete as we deem appropriate. As of now, there are no such floaters in the system.

A good thing for this gig is that Joe signed off wide open, so now I can render him a dual with a rather life-like palette. That makes for more interesting session reviews.

Joe's dual now looks kind of like the guy in the Scream painting. The ratio of the cranial surface area to the bottom half of his head is inordinately high.

He has a tall face and something about his head juts out.

But hey it's close enough, I got him done, as a draft at any rate.

On the other hand, this glitch girl who calls herself Heidi, we don't know who exactly she is, or even where she is at now.

So she will have to start out as a shadowy stick in the blow, till we find her for real and get her commitment for a more faithful render, if ever.

But I can of course play around with the shadows on the stick figure, oh yes. She's got a stash of botnets in her fishnets, oh yeah.

Yes, there she blows.

Now it is an experience.

God's blood ...

The interesting thing about the Conch is that it has features for perspective shift from person to person, or rather from dual to dual, to be exact. For this take, to start it up I slipped in the perspective of my dual. Let's see how it swivels along as we go.

On top of all this, the Conch has badass machine learning skills. If you have a petty habit for example, your conch blow persona will experience 'special effects' that enhance the context of that specific habit, as a measure of personalization.

In my case, I have this habit of running my knuckles against my face every now and then. My conch persona can sense when one such run is about to occur, and throws in corresponding sensory special effects within the context of any conch session I am in. So, whenever I have the headset on, and I happen to run my knuckle along my cheek or nose, the rendering in the session picks it up real-time, and my conch-dual (from whose perspective I am viewing the occurrence) will see special effects in the rendering, corresponding to how my hand moves.

So, roughly along those coordinates where my hand is moving, the conch session will see shimmer and glow and flashes and things like that, sort of like bioluminescence from sundry flora and fauna in the wake of a dolphin that jumps out of the water.

This feature adds a personal touch, and it is supposed to psychologically help ensure that you will identify with what your dual crunches on your behalf. This is per Bonar's design. The bastard knew his stuff, no doubt about that. It is this kind of machine learning based value proposition that ensures that the Conch will continue to remain a going concern. People dig it.

Who would have thought that applying Measure Theoretical techniques such as Support Vector Machine methods and Stochastic Gradient Descent calculations and affinity characterizations of probability distributions, to Machine Learning problems, would lead to business applications and even an actual honest to goodness marketable app!

Now see, this gig for instance is a prime indicator that my business is starting to really take off.

Well I'm not complaining. I'm a happy camper.

I do feel a bit uneasy reaping the benefits of this intellectual property though, considering that one of the founders namely Bonar is AWOL and his apportioned profits will remain unaccounted for, potentially indefinitely. Once things started to move forward with the Conch I tried quite hard to trace him, but to no avail.

With Emmy, it is fine; she is going to get what's hers when the time is right. We are just giving each other space right now, especially since things got a bit weird the last time she was plugged into a conch gig.

It's not a big deal though, not all that weird. Just the usual thing. I was hot for her, and she was hot for Bonar.

I can't say I blame her. Bonar had the air of a Polynesian prince with a bunch of islands at his behest, and he could charm the pants off any girl.

But he used to maintain a certain distance all the time, letting the mystery around him simmer. Nobody could get really close to him, not even Emmy.

And then one fine day he just vanished. Somehow, no one took note of it for a good while, and then gradually other things fell into place and he became a memory.

Once Bonar decamped, Emmy and I we tried working on some partner gigs, but there was awkwardness. So then she moved on.

I've of course made occasional remittances to her account, based on rough calculations of inflow. So far it has only been pocket change. Once the ROI starts to *really* show for the Conch we are going to properly reconcile anyway, and she knows that.

She's a strange girl, reclusive to the extreme in one vein, but at the same time very much impulsive in her relationships and physically expressive.

All right, enough with the memory lane. I've got to crunch this thing now, Joe's blow.

Crunch the countable first, and then the uncountable.

There is something soporific and out-of-body about the Conch experience, but I can't quite pin it down. I guess it's a trip, basically.

Whether I am by myself, or even when there is someone who is in a session and with me in my igloo, we stay awake and no one ever nods off, however long it takes. But there is a shared dreamlike state we get into, that transcends the typical conscious states of mind.

There are worlds nestled within the Conch. I'd recommend it for you as well, to try out a conch solution sometime.

The Conch runs on a peer to peer cloud share infrastructure or some such thing. I have only peripheral knowledge of that stuff. Bonar and Emmy set it all up, and the machinery is sufficiently self-aware that it keeps going pretty much on its own. On my part, I just work the math. The machinery of it is a background aspect for me most of the times.

Man, I'm really grooving on Heidi's shadow stick figure. She's sure got the moves.

The Early Days

Oh those were pioneer days indeed, truly frontier times. You could almost feel the wagon wheel dust, and hear the splintering sound of the flint tools chipping away at the forge somewhere around the block. Yes, life was quintessential back then.

All around, a lot was new and much was changing.

Not everything was hunky dory though. The backdrop all over the world was grim, given the ever increasing magnitude of environmental disasters and situations of political unrest across the board. The times were at crossroads in many ways. Doomsday prophets on the streets were gaining currency by the day.

On that front, there is no respite, even up to now. As the years go by, the elements of horror in the world continue to proliferate and persist. But especially during that time, it was particularly horrifying.

Maybe there is an element of morbidity in the consideration, but this grimness itself was possibly a key reason as to why the times back then were so raunchy. Accordingly, they were also fertile for crackpot inventors and startup companies, since the scene was always expanding along the fringes.

Anyway, at about that time I was doing some sideline contract work for Beacon at their Cupertino location, looking for a break from the measly assistantships and such limiting aspects of the post doc way of life.

One fine day, over some coffee at the cafeteria, when I was explaining measure theory to a colleague as a possible conceptual framework for business technology decisions, a woman at an adjacent table turned sharply to look at us.

"Why do we need measure theory for business applications? Seems to me you are trying to force two disparate domains together," my colleague, whose name was Chris something or the other, was voicing an opposing opinion.

"For starters, it is a foundation layer for probability theory as well as integral calculus, and both of those have applications galore for business enterprises," I started out with my reply.

And then the conversation went into some detail, over the course of the coffee.

"Pardon me for interjecting and I don't mean to be rude," said the same blonde woman who was seated at the table next to us, "but I couldn't help overhearing and I don't think the measure you are referring to is Hausdorff. It doesn't seem to be invariant under isometries." She was slight of frame, with sharp features. Once I looked across at her, I had to pull myself back with force. She sure could hold attention.

That was how I met Emmy Haken.

We asked her to join our table, my colleague and I, and the conversation then really took flight. She said she didn't have a formal math background, but seemed to know a heck of a lot.

"I'm still not sold on the value proposition of measure theory for business purposes," Chris persisted.

"Well, look at it this way," I said. "When you want to solve a problem analytically, if the problem is represented by what are mathematically known as *nice* curves, then regular calculus is sufficient."

Looking across at Emmy, I could see her perk up in anticipation.

"But when the curves that are under consideration are complicated," I continued, "you need measures."

Emmy laughed. "I sense a hint of a dirty mind there," she responded, "but I have to agree with what you said."

It took some time for us to lose Chris, and then for a while Emmy and I were thick as thieves.

She is a Montana girl, straight from the bluffs.

The two of us, we got real close for a bit. I managed to reach a point where I got my hand on her knee, and was maybe just a hair's breadth away from going down on *my* knee in turn and asking her to be mine, and just then Bonar happened.

Everything changed, everything became different. The strange thing is that I remember the state of tranquility that was upon us all.

I could see immediately that she felt right at home with Bonar, soon as he showed up. It was as though a turkey buzzard had landed on to a cottonwood tree.

Emmy was head over heels for him at first sight itself, and that too *just when* I was about to close in and make my move, but still I felt no animosity. I was blissful as well, a participant in the moment. So too were the others in the cafeteria, I felt. Something momentous had descended upon us all.

He walked right over to where Emmy and I were, and introduced himself to us.

"You have good ideas," he said. "I have been following your posts and conversations, and I believe these kinds of solutions could be operationalized and provided as an offering to consumers. We can make this a revenue generating service."

"But these are basic concepts and simple things that we keep talking about," I questioned, "what is special about them that would make people want to consider them commercially? Even when I myself posit these ideas as having applicability to the business domain, I am only talking theoretically with an academic point of view.

Getting someone to actually pay money is a whole other thing."

"Think of yourself as a lightning rod, buddy," Bonar responded. I thought I could actually see bolts of lightning in his eyes while he was speaking. "Ideas that generate value are almost always simple and basic. You just have to draw the lightning and ground it. And in the process, siphon off the charge that you need."

"I do find the possibilities exhilarating," I said, "but how do we make the rubber hit the road?"

"Think thermodynamically," Bonar smiled. "All our industry is built on such thought. What is money? It is a representation of value. What is value? It is in turn a representation of the output product of a mechanical process, of some kind of a machine. There are parts to the machine, with individual as well as collective functions. These functions generate value, depending upon the user's needs. The understanding of these functions requires mathematics, and the thread within math that you are developing is a core one. It will tap into the value chain, trust me."

Well I mull on that.

"What kind of machines are you referring to?" Emmy asks him in the meanwhile.

"It could be anything," he says. "Even an Enterprise as a whole, from production line to sales and customer relations with underlying corporate functions, this entire structure can be considered to be one machine. Yes, corporations are machines, governments as well. The brands associated with these are machines on their own, a more fluid type though. At the same time, they are constituent parts of the base structure. Machines are everywhere, wherever people are. Humans are a product of nature, and machines are in turn human products. If we *get with the machine* so to speak, we can harvest the chain and the cycle, as per our needs."

We were completely mesmerized by his vision, Emmy and I, and started out on the project right away.

We then built an amazing thing.

It has three major components: the Quantum Compute, the Semiotics Parser, and the Experiential Interface.

The Experiential Interface would allow administrators, which basically meant me and Emmy, to input into the sessions and determine the user experience.

The Semiotics Parser would hermeneutically render meanings to the sessions based on the inputs from the users as well as from us as the administrators. The libraries it uses range from mythologies to urban dictionaries. The Inference Engine, with both Bayesian as well as non-Bayesian modes, is a sub-component of the Semiotics Parser.

The Quantum Compute would apply measures to those meanings, based on probability amplitude calculations. Bonar's depth of understanding of the Principle of Superposition was mind blowing. His insights have been critical to the whole thing.

Piece by piece, the Conch started to come together.

What disasters we used to deal with, huh. All three of us would perennially have frizzled hair. The VR headset was pretty much a mechanical bull in disguise.

Overall, the Nineties were rip roaring years, especially from 2097 to the turn of the century. It was almost as though *time* itself as an entity had figured that reaching the end of a century in our local terrestrial contexts warrants flamboyance, flourishes, and - grand gestures.

And correspondingly, during the build of the Conch it was quite the carnival for us. It was like a hallucinogenic experience.

Strips would peel off of rendered reality takes, and we'd have no idea how to fix that.

If say my conch dual was drinking a glass of water, suddenly my view from the VR console would show a coiled strip spring off, with sliced sections of the water glass, my hand, the sights on the street, the sky, all from different depth levels, and this springing slice would coil up and blank out, while the rest of the rendered reality across all those levels would merrily continue on along. It was highly unnerving.

Emmy was always quick to the rescue, ever the hard core engineer. And Bonar's designs were ingenious to the bone. He would always have a solution, for any problem that arose.

We built a beautiful thing. The Conch experience is something sublime. In a conch session, you can tilt, zoom, pan, drag, hold, and release … whatever helps you stay in the moment. We whipped up a frenzy of feature builds, threw in whatever we could think of. It just grew and grew, into a thing of beauty, the Conch.

Joe Blow

Indeed what a ride it has been, the past half-decade leading up to now, this topsy-turvy year 2102. I'm ever so sore, but still very much wired and on the go.

So much has happened along with the turn of the millennium. For one thing, the Julian and Gregorian calendars have arrived at coincidental days, although not sure if anyone is keeping track any more.

My academic path has taken quite a hit over these years though, so much so that now I've primarily become the Conch guy, doing some incidental post doc work on the side just as a fallback option and to keep the brain agile and fit in multiple ways. Life has a way of finding its own paths, huh. I don't really feel the pinch of not having become a mainstream academician, I must admit. It's all good, I'm happy to be the Conch guy.

That's enough reminiscing now, here's Joe calling me, time to swing back to the current moment.

Just as I thought, he has laid down anchor at Big Sur. He wants to dig in into the blow at first chance.

He provides hardly a heads-up, says he is ten minutes away. Man, I hate shaving such close margins. I had suggested that we should meet at Moe's Alley in town, and ease into the plan from there. But no, he wants to dig right into it, just like an annoying kid.

And … here he is now. At least he is dressed up casual this time, Bermuda shorts and all, in contrast to how he had showed up last week. This is California, for goodness sake. I guess for the previous visit he must have considered it to be a business matter for signing the contract, hence his formal getup that time. I find it strange when people partition their wardrobes for different situations. For me, it is tee shirt and jeans and up and about and that's it, whatever the occasion.

"I'm camping at Pfeiffer State Park," he says, grinning. "I got my personal camp gear drone-delivered. I can rig up an awesome bivouac you know. We should try camping together some time."

"That's nice. Emmy used to spend a lot of time there when she was stationed here in California," I reply.

She has been in many roles at Beacon, over the years.

The Data Science crew for Beacon is based out of California. When she was dealing with them a lot, she used to spend her time on the Pacific Coast Highway. The New York office is where they chop the financials and the associated enterprise systems. The boiler-room work happens in India for the most part.

"As a matter of fact, she now works in the Security Division at Beacon. I think I might pull her in for this one, bro," I tell Joe further, as he settles into a chair in the study.

"Why do we need a bouncer? We are not going to have much time for partying while we're on this case, dude," he says.

"I am referring to IT Security, that's her line of work," I clarify.

Ah, he nods sagely.

It *is* a party house though, Beacon Inc. as a whole. I guess it comes with the territory considering the stuff that it purveys as a company, so I can't say I blame him for his assumption.

Dude doesn't even want a drink this time. He's ready to hit it right off.

"OK man, bring it on, I'm ready to blow," he says.

Whoa … fella.

What can I tell him? There's such a thing as gestation. It is better to take the time needed. Also, once your toes are in this water, you've crossed the point of no return as regards to your identity boundary. It definitely merits proper cogitation before making the move. Even for repeat customers like Joe, what was captured regarding his personality and identity in the previous round need not necessarily mean that he is not incurring further vulnerability with this one, so it is not like one has already been there and done that so let's move on already. Each deal has its own seal.

"Emmy and I identify with a Bob Dylan quote," is all I can think of. "You know, he was the guy I had been telling you about when we had first met at Chariot three years ago. According to him, '*privacy is something that you can sell, but can't buy back*'."

I find it a most appropriate quotation, to caution people before they get into a conch session. What they commit to, to their duals, is way bigger than what they might have thought it was, and it is out of their hands once they are in session. The monster has taken birth, and there is no route back to the womb. The state of mind with which they enter into the session makes all the difference.

Joe doesn't seem to be concerned, just like anybody else these days. People actually *want* to put it all out there, any which way.

I shouldn't get too worked up about it I guess.

But who knows, maybe *I am* the one who has the finger on the right pulse about this concern, and most of the world is off on a tangent. Even Emmy is on the same page as me.

I'm a throwback to more personal and private times, psychologically. It probably goes back to my Garo Hills tribal roots that I am content enough with just the overall cosmos in the fore and me in tune with it in the background, and no need to impose on anyone else unless situation warrants it. The Machines of these days on the other hand get everyone to hang it all out on their sleeves, right at the outset. I cringe at the thought, usually, for any such undertaking that I myself ever need to go through. But the Conch did suck me in though, and I've thereby strung myself out there, along with the rest of the subscriber base, in the cyberspace of the Conch.

It's weird, the Conch has more of an element of personal exposure for the consumer than for us as the administrators, and it is *our* product. But we seem to be the only ones bothered enough to raise the caution. The users are all fine with letting it all out.

Privacy … it sure has been a jaded notion, for quite a while now.

No one cares for it, most of the times.

Then again, when some malevolence or threat starts to loom, all of a sudden everyone ducks for cover, people got bat crazy to dig themselves into pseudo-privacy fallout shelters.

The one other case where people *do* pay heed to it is for side alley dalliances and such likes, which is why Beacon caters to that security need so much. But all of that security is for after the fact, the privacy waivers have already occurred.

Enough ranting now, I really need to shake this habit.

The user input process is quite involved and extended, it takes hours to complete.

In the meantime, Joe casually asks me a couple of more things about Emmy since I seem to be mentioning her so very often I guess, and then jumps on straight to what he has been obsessing about.

"Sign me in now, man," he says excitedly.

I know, right?

But hey, he is the customer.

I still have to set stuff up and rig the jig for him though, it's not just about his inputs and sign-offs. The machine needs various input heat energies for its Carnot cycle; the beast needs to be fed many meals. For this gig specifically, the Experience Interface of the Conch had to process what all goes in L.A. in the summertime, for goodness sake! Have you ever been there in the summer? You can't just dip a toe into the water just like that, for this kind of an experience. Correspondingly, the starting up of an instance needs ramp-up time too.

Meanwhile I try to get to know Joe's state of mind on this a bit.

"Why are you so hot to trot on this one, buddy?" I ask him. "I know this glitch thing is technologically speaking a big deal, but at a personal level, why does it matter so much to you? A street incident ruffled you, I get it, but why not let it go since you seem to be hitting a wall in the chase? Also, from a money angle the risk can't be all that significant for you? So is it really worth it?"

Man, I shot out a whole slew of questions there.

"What can I say? I'm a spirit brother to Ahab," Joe replies. "You know, the guy who had the whale eating from his hand. Not just any hunk of blubber, I'm talking about *the* whale."

I'm not sure what the final tally was between Moby Dick and Ahab, but I know what Joe means. Although it is to be noted, that what the white whale was eating from was Ahab's leg, not his hand.

"As long as you don't call me Ishmael," I say.

"Ah no, mate. When you are on my ship you'd be a first officer, not a deckhand," he replies.

I'd be just fine swabbing decks actually, way less hassles.

Anyway, let's get on with the business on hand.

OK, buddy, here you go.

I set him up with the primary headset, and I myself settle into one of the co-pilot shadow viewers.

From the co-pilot view, I see the contrasting façade of the strip mall building show up in the render.

<Pan in … and lock in on Joe's dual's perspective … and there, incoming, are his thoughts …>

Inglewood! Man, I dig this town.

I particularly like this convenience store here in this strip mall. They've got unbelievable jerky …

Holy moly, just look at that chick! She is sizing me up too. Of course she is. Who wouldn't? I'm the cat's meow.

That's it? Honey, I warrant a proper look!

Why is she peering into the alleyway at the side of the Laundromat now?

Never mind, I see a beacon lock, that's all I need, so let me reach in. "Hey there, sugar bush."

What the hell?

<Co-Pilot View>

The girl does the swivel act, and has him at her mercy.

</Co-Pilot>

Mother of God, I am staring at death in the face.

"I'm sure you've got your cojones in working order. But I have a pair of my own, you know," she is saying to me. "I carry them in my purse; they go by the names of Smith and Wesson."

She packs serious heat, oh crap.

While she is talking, out of the corner of my eye I see a fellow at the other end of the alleyway. He has a look of manic urgency. Damn, he seems to be pointing a gun at her. I swear under my breath, and pull her in.

Jesus, she takes her own gun out and takes aim from cover, and just shoots the guy, calmly and casually, like it is routine business.

"I should take you down as well. Nobody gropes me, ever …, nobody, unless I ask for it", she says to me, with a slight smile. "But I'll let it go, since you helped save my life. And don't say I'm not generous. I'll even give you a little extra on top. If you're ever at a shampoo dunk, tell them Heidi sent you," so saying, she hands me a card.

"So what's a nice girl like you ..." I start to say.

<Co-Pilot View>

Okay, Joe's panic level has gone down, at least reduced enough for him to be able to continue his prowl.

Actually, it seems more likely to be a post facto element of bravado that he is injecting into the blow. Let him have some fun now, we'll have to work out some edit boundaries later on. A bit of fantasy spin is okay here and there, so long as it works within the measure.

</Co-Pilot>

"Don't be fooled by my looks, little boy. I'm from Monterrey, Mexico," she says. "Coming to L.A. is like a sabbatical for me, even when I'm on the job. It's a walk in the park."

Okay, then.

"What about you? What's your story?" she asks me.

"I'm a sales guy for Chariot. I am beta testing for some new product features. Motels are where my test beds are, literally," I tell her, pointing to the adjacent hovel. "It's not bad, just different from what I used to do before at Beacon. I was a salesman there."

"Ah, just as I thought, you're a man whore," she says.

"On the contrary my dear, my Beacon stint virtually makes me a man of cloth," I hit back.

She smiles more freely now, and checks her watch and walks off down the sidewalk along the alley, casually hopping over the corpse along the way.

"Watch yourself now. Just because I got my back turned doesn't mean you get a ring side show. If I get a bad feeling about you, I'll shuck your eyes out, just like pearls from oysters," is her shot at me as she exits.

<Co-Pilot View>

Joe is in a daze, maybe I need to shake him up a bit? Ah there he is.

</Co-Pilot>

What the...? This is nuts, I'm going to call on the moose.

"Dude, why do you call me that?" the moose, my inspiration, steps out of the Laundromat place.

"Hey, fella, there were some Greek plays back at school I was a part of, they kept calling on you all the time, so I figured you'd be fun to hang out with," I tell him. He should know, pretty much everyone calls on him!

"You poor sod, they were calling on the muse!" he says.

Ah, potayto / potahto …

<Co-Pilot View>

There you go. I managed to modulate my dual on to this freak imaginary buddy of Joe's. He has a full on song and dance routine with this fella, wow. They must have been friends since childhood.

It is time now to morph from the moose and become my dual for this gig.

</Co-Pilot>

"Hey Joe, you better get out of here before either the cops or the cartel thugs arrive in force," the moose says, while transforming in a weird way into this guy.

Hey, I know him, he is the Conch fellow!

Powering down, okay let's step out now.

The moose thing is a kludge, but we'll fix as we go. It all got built off of the inputs he had provided up front. The machine taps into all his lobes, the parietal, occipital, and along on all the way down the cerebro-spinal network. The accessory themes in the session are all his. Yes sir, the imaginary buddy is not of my making, the onion is all in Joe's head and vicinities. I only patched and modulated my dual on to the narrative that's all, and helped with the peeling.

Joe sure has had a good session, overall. It totally shows on his face. Reliving experiences this way seems to hit a spiritual nerve for people, they come out rejuvenated.

Indeed, he is grinning.

"What the hell?" he says. "You went loco, bro! You turned her into Jessica Rabbit! That's good and all in a way I guess, but the girl I'm talking about is wholesome and homely. In fact, that was what got me hooked in the first place. I know she's got this underworld side, but she's still got that girl next door look for me. Bring her in proper, Vibe!"

Man, he is picky.

Oh well, I'll redo the render once we find her, and if she signs, maybe. As for me, I'm good with how it is.

Site Visit

I believe we have it now, the conch instance.

Joe has taken short-term root at Big Sur, pretty much, and keeps popping in and out, as and when I let him. I've never had a client be so involved in the draft stages. It is bothersome, personal space wise, but at the same time, it has helped with the authenticity of the conch instances, no denying.

The current state of the take is fairly good; both Joe and I feel so. Further takes will get us to better measures. I have a name for it, '*Joe's Blow*'. He does this weird thing with his face upon hearing the name, a mix of a grin and a grimace. I don't think he likes it.

I don't care, that's my name for it.

"So what's next?" Joe asks.

Well, we have to go by the measures. That's what the blows are for.

So let's take one now.

This is the part of the process that gives me the greatest thrill, when I apply Carathéodory's extension theorem to a given conch take. I identify the countable collections of sets in a real life situation, take the summation of the volumes of each such, and then determine the greatest lower bound (also known as the infimum) - oh, it is such an exquisite joy. Voila, we have a measure.

What once used to be considered a domain of pure math, now has marketplace applications. Such is the way of progress.

The outtake we get from the measure is that Joe and I need to visit the site of the occurrence, to *get real* so to speak. That is the message from the Conch.

I offer up a ride on my beat-up station wagon, the Kaiser Dragon Reborn, although hitting Southern California on it from here would be a nutcase job, to be honest.

"Do you have any idea how ugly the sig alerts on the 405 are these days?" " Joe says.

I've no idea what he is talking about, some SoCal argot I guess.

Thankfully, he has a better idea, a Toucan option. I've never flown on one of those before.

"How often do you visit L.A.?" Joe asks me.

"I've only been there a handful of times," I reply.

"You're kidding me! Once we're done with our task, I'll show you the real city, bro," he says graciously. "No tourist stuff. You don't want to end up at the Hollywood and Highland Intersection at the wrong time, or eat Pink's hot dogs or things like that. You have to properly experience the City of Lights."

We drive up to a helipad in Opal Cliffs where he has parked his sleek dark orange Dagger. It's a signature Joe Kerr item all right. Just look at that embossed license tag for starters. Every section of the body has a character of its own.

The bugger is real fancy. Daggers are top of the line Toucans, he tells me. I can believe it.

The Toucan, from what I looked up before we set out on this trip, is a form of high-end transportation, of category Autonomous Aerial Vehicle, or AAV as they are called. On top of that, per Joe, of all the makes and models of Toucans, the Daggers are the most expensive. This AAV concept started out as a bike combined with a jet ski that could go airborne, and then Ehang built the one-passenger machines which were the earliest of this category of flying machines, and now it has evolved to a point where two can fly (hence the name Toucan!) at upwards of a hundred miles per hour, at near earth altitudes. The traffic control is all done via instrumentation, mostly from centralized control hubs, but some fine tuning decisions for trajectory optimization remain with the pilot.

These urban types, they are into all this kind of stuff, and I don't know who or what keeps coming up with it all, Santa Claus maybe. As for me, I'm a backwaters fella myself and happy with the simple things usually. But I do enjoy the flashy rides and all, as and when situations arise.

His machine has a name carved on it – The Pequod.

"I know where that comes from," I grin at him.

"Yeah man, that whaler is my spirit brother, so as a gesture of solidarity I name my ride for his," he says, leading me in through the gull-wing door. As we get inside, I realize that the instrumentation panel and the rest of the interior elements show much stronger character than the exterior, personality even. I am impressed.

"What does it run on?" I ask.

"Aviation fuel," he replies. "There used to be other options that were preferred due to the environmental considerations in earlier days but then the graveyards for all the Lithium Ion and Lead Acid and Nickel Hydride etc. started to become a challenge to manage as well, so the industry has moved back to old fashioned gas, at least for now."

The Pequod's visor glass has some accumulated precipitation on it. It almost instantaneously clears, at the press of a button.

"So tell me more about the Conch, how it works," Joe asks, once we have settled into the ride.

"You need to understand measure theory first," I respond. "Measures are intuitive things; they are extensions of the concepts of length, area, and volume. For abstract geometric entities ('nice' regions from a mathematical point of view) such basic measures suffice, but for real world problems, it gets hairier. Enter The Conch. It can perform the corresponding exercise on real world situations, similar to how integral calculus helps us get the area or volume of one to three dimensional 'nice' regions."

"Give me an example, that's how I usually plug into concepts. Theoretical details go flying by my head," he says.

I can actually visualize that happening, like how spacecraft are catapulted along their trajectory by celestial bodies. Vroom ... there goes another abstract concept, flying past Joe's noggin.

"OK, let's take a real world case," I propose. "How about comparing roundabouts and four way stops?"

"You mean on the ground, right?" Joe says, rhetorically I hope.

"Yeah, buddy," I reply. "I can't really see how the concept would apply up here. Unless I am missing something and we do have those mechanisms in the near earth airspace as well? Also, I doubt if submarine traffic has them either. Anyway, yes, on the ground." Man, I suck at sarcasm.

"Coming to the point," I continue, "at roundabouts there are possibly uncountable options as to who goes first, whereas with four way stops the options are countable. Let's start understanding measure from this context."

Using this example, we hammer measure theory a bit. We analyze countable and uncountable sets that arise from this case study for both options, and it starts to get real tricky. I throw in a dose of the Banach-Tarski paradox in the context of the probability densities of collision occurrences in each option, and that messes up Joe's head even further. "Enough," he says.

The Toucan is pretty much autonomous once the initial settings are made, but there are a few things that do require the pilot's undivided attention during flight. So we take a break from this discussion and focus on the journey.

As we cruise over the land and ocean, the view is fantastic of course. First, we fly over Monterey Bay and along the coast up to Carmel-by-the-Sea, and then take a few back and forth swings over the Los Padres forests while still making our way south to San Luis Obispo. Not sure why, but I guess the route is determined by NEA (Near Earth Autonomy) optimization algorithms, and there are quite a few pinball trajectories for any given itinerary, across various geospatial parcels I'm guessing, that are designed per some NEA logic. Finally, the route stabilizes into something closer to a geodesic, and I start getting a sense of the destination.

But as we approach the Sepulveda Pass vicinity, there is a sudden jerk and some blinding flashes, and we both swear at the same time.

"Damn it, how did that happen? I had checked and set all the route protocol properties," Joe fumes. "It's your fault," he grumbles at me. "You and your stupid measure theory example and all that talk about collisions, just look what it led to."

I'm scared. The dome is spinning like crazy.

"Don't worry, we're safe," Joe says. "The spinning of the dome is some kind of gyroscopic mechanism to contain any potential turbulent motion of the unit."

I am getting nauseous, but just about manage to hold it. That would be nasty, having to lug a barf bag for the remainder of the journey.

"How can this be a collision? We're on our own here, where is the other Toucan?" I ask, once the thing stabilizes a bit.

"The impact gets identified on the echo-location network, the other guy need not be within sight," Joe says.

The Toucan network operates on an electromagnetic echo-locator mechanism. The instrumentation on the unit is mainly for that purpose.

Now that this incident has occurred, we are fixed on auto-pilot, and are automatically routed to a spot where it can all be sorted out.

We get pulled over to a ledge on the Santa Monica Mountains. For me, the view is further accentuated by the fresh air, but Joe's anger at this whole situation is still white hot, he is not into the surroundings. The other Toucan is already there. The guy at the helm is also swearing and muttering curse words under his breath.

We start walking towards each other. We can see the Getty Center on the other side of the road.

"The parasites will start to gather now," Joe grumbles.

Momentarily, a tow truck arrives, with the name *Royal Auto Collision* on their logo. A fellow with a semi-aquatic look to him, looking kind of like a newt maybe, is driving it.

He is most commiserating, acts real familiar, and calls everyone brother. He introduces himself as Munir.

He has a loping gait while he walks back and forth between the two grounded machines.

"That is a strange way of walking," I comment.

"Yes, a lot of people are starting to walk like that these days," says Joe.

Lanny Wayne has started this thing too, this lurching and loping way of walking. Lanny is the principal investigator for the post doc work I'm currently doing at UCSC, on some problems in quasi-periodic orbits. As a person, he is an obnoxious piece of work, and this lurching and loping body language heightens that aspect of his quite a bit. Lancelot Wayne, as it is he has such a sallow unsavory look, and a hollow and shallow personality. Totally unlike the knight of yore whose first name he carries, there is no trace of gallantry in Lanny Wayne's fiber. He is just a crotchety old man taking out the grim effects of his internally imbalanced fluid equations on the world in general. And yes, he shows this same loping and lurching behavior.

Indeed, this messed up gait is becoming a bit of a pattern amongst several people, and getting to be rather concerning.

As the human species, over the ages we have been riding on so many patterns as we have evolved.

I guess if we look at our life on earth with a zoom lens so to speak, what does our story look like? We have evolved from eukaryotic roots and reached a certain biped nature and boom, here we are. But how are we handling the apex status though?

We're still changing, all the time, and not necessarily in good ways. Back in the early digital days, people used to end up with deformed postures due to stooping on to devices all the time. The human race fought back and managed to contain that regressive tendency to an extent, with focus on ergonomics. Initially this loping and lurching seemed to be just another such thing, the effect of some lifestyle causes. But now, as regards this gait and associated behavioral traits, something much more concerning seems to be underlying. It's not even a classified disease yet, but I get the feeling that we humans are going irredeemably bad with this one. One wonky gene expression and the whole house of cards that is the current human state could come down crumbling, and we'll have to go line up along with the dinosaurs, in the annals of evolution. This loping gait might well be such a risk. Ah, I don't know, I'm too pessimistic sometimes.

Okay, head, stop wandering, focus back to the here and now.

"These ugly bastards," Joe says, referring to the tow truck crew, "they should be called *Rogue Auto Collusion* instead of the name they go by. They are the worst kind of parasites, waiting in the shadows for the pieces of scrap and salvage from the vehicles of unfortunate folks like us who fall into their traps."

"Did you ever run into them before?" I ask.

"A friend of mine had a bad collision, and his Dagger had to be totaled," Joe elaborates. "He wanted to carve out portions of it and convert them into furniture, as a keepsake. He signed over the papers to these guys, trusting that they would cut the body and hand over the material to him, based on the verbal understanding that he would pay them for the cut material at the time of handover. But they never did hand it over. The likely reason would be that the scrap value of the vehicle (which was already in their hands as per the signed over papers) would be comparable to the value of what he would have paid them minus the labor cost of doing the cutting, so they just decided to skip doing the work. Once they had the papers in their hands, they just kept on giving him the runaround. He chased them many times, in person as well as over the phone, but they would slither and slip away every occasion, and in frustration he finally gave up."

"Yeah man, sounds like a nasty thing all right," I concur.

"These parasites don't value human sentiment at all," Joe fumes. "They are greedy for quick profit even if the means are unethical. They just collect their scrap and salvage from the scenes of accidents even when it doesn't ethically belong to them. They have no compunction about breaking the impacted people's hearts in the process, and the system is rigged in their favor. The insurance companies, the cops, they're all in on it. There are so many terrible things in this world, man. At some level, it is not just parasitic, it gets out and out predatory, if you look at a similar setup that exists in the so-called healthcare industry for instance. But this rogue auto collusion is my pet peeve."

In our case right now though, the impact is rather minor and so we don't need to go to their auto body shop. Joe heaves a sigh of relief.

The diagnostics have been completed, and both our Toucans have been released. So now we set off to

Inglewood, and beyond, wherever this conch quest takes us. Who knows where this gig is leading us to, come to think of it? This is the most open ended assignment I've ever signed up for.

As we approach the location, there is a fog upon L.A. The buildings look like ghosts, and the people around are just like memories and past sensations.

It's not just the fog though; I've been feeling this way ever since we started out on the Conch project, right from the prototype days. I have a gut feeling that there is correlation between this downer state of mine and the way the Conch is evolving. Too many head games with this thing, basically.

The Toucan drops us off at a vantage point by means of a ladder, and it then automatically makes its way over towards the nearest garage, to remain there till invoked again later.

Joe calls for a cab, to get us over to Century Boulevard. The city we see along the way is as much of a nut house as I've always felt it to be.

A part of the street has construction work barricades set up, but there is no work going on. The street kids have ingeniously converted that section into a skateboard hub. Our cab slows down till the kids move out of the way, and then we continue forward. One hot shot rider on roller power blades navigates around us and the other cars, and zips by at a hundred miles per hour or so, just for the short stretch of a block or two.

On the sidewalk there is a jolly and jaunty lady firmly holding onto her partner, quite likely a husband, by the crook of his elbow. She is talking rather animatedly. As they approach a puddle, for herself she deftly sidesteps it. But as to her partner, he is screwed. There is another guy on his other side walking alongside of the two of them, and that other fellow is as it is dodging various situations of pavement peril, all while precariously slobbering away on a hot dog.

The poor husband guy has no choice. With a resolute look on his face, he resignedly plows his way through the puddle, woefully bemoaning, "this has already happened twice this month."

Slices of city life - we pass more people, make some more shady turns. Suddenly, a couple of thugs pop out of the alley at us, and both Joe and I are staring down the barrels of a gun each. The thugs have grotesque masks over their faces.

I am scared witless. Joe on the other hand, is the boss of the situation. He brings up his left arm facing towards him close to his sternum and makes a fist like gesture, sort of like wresting out his heart and putting it on the table. It is a full-fledged mime act with the entire body in on the show, not just your run of the mill gang sign. The thugs reluctantly back off, with an even more pronounced lurching and loping than what we saw with the people at the collision resolution site back there. This thing is becoming rampant, so many lopers all over.

As this pair is backing off, one of them sees a cat crossing the street, and shoots it down just to vent out his rage.

Evil is usually not that far away. We drift amidst desolation all the time. The whole world is shot to pieces at this juncture of history. I do wonder sometimes though if it's always been like this. Who knows?

We remain silent and still for a long while, mourning the poor cat.

Then we commence our further journey, a somber walk.

Eventually we reach the strip mall, our site of action.

"What was that all about, all those hand gestures?" I ask.

"The streets are all about relationships," Joe explains. "The more you live here, the more you belong."

I'm sure glad he's on my side. "Man, the masks on those guys were ugly," I say.

"They are respiro-filter masks," Joe clarifies. "If you live long enough in L.A., you'll see the value proposition in such things, the air is going to the skunks here. There are all kinds of faces and all kinds of masks these days."

We look around the place, the strip mall. The Byzantine touch seems rather out of place in the context of its environs, but hey, someone must have liked it to have designed it so.

I then ask Joe to grab some media shots of me at the exact site of the event, so that I can bake them in into further conch takes.

We spend some more time absorbing the atmosphere here and in the neighborhood. Before we know it, it is late evening.

"Let's park at my place for tonight, and then we can continue the work tomorrow," Joe says.

I hesitate and tell him I'll take a greyhound and he can catch up tomorrow, but he insists. He is an affable chap. My problem is that I'm not. Tomorrow it will be my turn in Santa Cruz, and once I've accepted his hospitality, I won't be able to shunt him off to Big Sur or wherever. The good angel over my shoulder bonks me on the head and tells me to be a good person and do the civil thing, and I comply.

So we then head over to Joe's house just to wind down for the night. We will fly back in his Toucan in the morning, to continue at the igloo.

I didn't realize that his apartment complex is actually *in* the ocean, a structure built just off of where the Roundhouse Aquarium is at the pier, sufficiently distant to allow room for the people at the beach. Some folks get to their homes from the Manhattan Beach Pier directly, via simple water scooters. For others with larger sized and land based motor vehicles, there is a ferry dock a bit further south from off the Strand.

We get off the cab and take a ferry ride, looking over the side at the churning waters.

Ennyk

Back at my home the next day, under the auspices of the igloo, we now crunch the context further. This gig is starting to feel like a whale's blowhole. Fitting, I guess, given Joe's Moby Dick obsession.

The next output advice of the Conch instance, coming right out of the left field, is to tune into a genre-set of music denoted as N-IC, pronounced Ennyk, expanding as Non-Inertial Composites.

We're both left scratching our heads as to why, but so it is. I look it up.

The common ancestor for this set of genres of music was a mid-last-century genre called heavy metal which a lot of hard hat folks had happened to get into at one time. Of course, over time these categories of listeners moved through many different forms. A typical direction for a lot of them was industrial forms of music, and given the locations where N-IC became prevalent, it ended up being basically whatever the Maquiladora workforce was into, at times it even experimented with variants of canciones rancheras. But the tag *non-inertial composites*, was a tip of the hat at that old name *heavy metal*.

The link to the girl we are chasing, is because according to the conch outtake, she is the Ennyk type, whatever that means.

Further Conch logic that has backed this advice is the surmise based conclusion that over time the cartel has hooked into this music network in various ways, and is using the N-IC roadshows as diversions for other nefarious activities. Since the glitch girl is manifestly cartel, QED.

I'm not fully sold on this take, but maybe while we go rub shoulders with the N-IC junta, some clues might surface for the issue we have on hand. Sure why not, we can give it a try.

A more specific instruction pops out now – we are exhorted to go meet with Marlon Jones, a UCLA scholar of social mores, and ask him about his thesis. From there a path and next steps will emerge. This is getting weird now.

Anyway, we've committed to seeing it through, so here we go.

Another Toucan trip, and we're back again in L.A. I think we'll have to work out a Mobile Conch option for this gig till we find the girl, these ping pong trips back and forth across California are starting to feel inefficient.

The Toucan drops us off at a parking lot from where Joe brings out some fancy branded car. He keeps telling me things like 6-speed, 4.2 liters, and stuff. I'm only listening with half an ear.

"Nothing like stick shift on old fashioned gasoline, if you ask me," he says. I'm okay, whatever works for you, man.

We get on Highway 405 North, and after due wrestling with contending vehicles and finally squeezing ourselves out at the destination exit, reach UCLA.

Marlon Jones was surprised at my request, but has graciously agreed to meet with us nonetheless. He has asked us to come over and meet him at the rim of the inverted fountain next to the Music Building in the University.

We reach there and among the crowd at the fountain, we see a man waving furiously at us.

"Professor Jones?" Joe extends a hand inquiringly, and the man grins hugely and nods his head in a vigorous affirmative.

It's him.

"I could sense that it is you, by how out of place you both look," he says.

He seems to be a sharp fellow, huh.

"Thank you for making the time to meet with us," I respond.

"Call me Marlon," he grins. "Now what can I do for you?"

"We are following an algorithm and have been instructed to seek you out per the same," I start out on trying to explain our quest. "We can get into the details as required, but for our immediate purposes, suffice it to say that the application whose instructions we are following has asked us to find out from you about your PhD thesis."

Marlon scratches his beard.

"Well, it has been many years since I earned my doctorate," he replies. "I'm more than happy to discuss what I remember about it of course. My thesis was on 'The Mimamsa of the *More Cowbell* Meme'".

"What does that mean?" Joe asks.

"Mimamsa is critical reflexive investigation," Marlon starts to expound. I am aware of the concept, it is a Sanskrit term.

"I was born in Upstate New York," he says. "Over the course of my life, I charted a South-Westerly course at different stages, and finally here you see me now, at UCLA. Along this trip of my life line, I have observed a lot of in-your-face discordance and dissonance in the way things are in general, in the world that we live in. The scholar in me started to delve into the memetics of it all. A comedy sketch from a long time ago used the term *more cowbell* to showcase this thing, and that has evolved as a meme into so many forms, over the years."

"How does it relate to N-IC?" Joe asks. He wants to cut to the chase.

"Ah, Ennyk," Marlon muses. "Sure, it ties in. Everything relates back to *More Cowbell*, buddy. Ennyk started out referencing heavy metal, and then traversed a whole taxonomy therein; thrash, groove, black, doom, folk, grind, core, progressive, industrial, speed, stoner, post, power, death, glam, gothic, extreme, crust, punk, ah I can't even keep track really. There are hosts of musical genres associated with Ennyk now, mostly of industrial tinges but not necessarily referencing that old concept of metal. That was why some smart alec coined the term *non-inertial* as a generalization of heavy, and *composites* as a generalization of types of material, which could include metals but have other elements from the periodic table, and compounds, polymers, what not. That is what Ennyk is."

Then Marlon really digs in into his domain and takes us along on a magic trip. The ensuing discussion is spellbinding, with dizzying twists and turns of musical and pop culture history. We glean a world of insights from him. Gradually I start to see the connection between the social contexts within which people like the glitch girl lead their lives, and this Ennyk scene.

Marlon is a real jolly fellow. I'm glad we met.

We say goodbye to him and continue with our quest. We need to infiltrate the strata of society where she would likely be at. So hey, why not chase the music, at any rate we'll have fun along the way.

This gig now, Joe's Blow, seems annoyingly trivial at one level. At the same time, there is something seemingly intractable about it, infuriatingly so, and hard to pin down. Honestly speaking, a clear direction has not really emerged. We're kind of drifting, and hoping things will fall into place.

One thing is for sure, it will strain my capacity and mental resources, since we're pushing into lots of new territory here. I need backup.

Emmy is not easy to talk to or even to reach in any other way, these days. Well I guess I was a jerk too, on quite a few occasions. I keep trying though, every now and then. We shared a heck of a lot of trench time and wrench time in the early days of the Conch, after all.

I ping her, and reach her voicemail as usual.

She is plugged into the boiler room work for Beacon these days, at Shahabad, in India.

The next day, the phone rings. What a surprise, this time she is actually returning my call! She says it would be great to catch up, but I would have to make the trip to where she is at, since she's got some critical things going on and cannot commit as to when she will be back in the USA.

Tango at Shahabad

So I head out to India to meet up with Emmy.

To my delight, she said she will meet me at Shamshabad airport, in Hyderabad City.

It has been so long.

All through the flight journey, whenever I close my eyes I see her face, fresh and bright. I really can't wait to see her in person again.

Sure enough, there she stands waiting for me at arrival. Her dusty hair is a shade of harvest gold.

I shoot for the lips but get the cheek. She is deft! So goes our tango, a portmanteau of touch and go. It's not as if she is averse to public display of affection either, she is a very physically expressive personality. But I somehow always end up with the short straw, a residual carry-over from our early Conch days I guess. Well, hey, I can't compare with Bonar the debonair fellow, and she can't seem to shake off that constraint as regards our equation. Too bad ... but it is okay, I'll settle for the friend zone with her, as long as we are able to reconnect.

"Nice to see you, Vibhu," she says.

Hell now, no one has called me that since ma died. Back then in Cupertino, Emmy used to call me Vibe, just like everyone else. I guess she has really plugged into local mores here, including the sensibilities and sounds of Indian names.

Yes she sure has gone native and with vengeance at that. I can see it in the way she deals with the people as we make our way out of the airport. She is a rough rider all right. We are heading over to the transit option that works for what she has in mind for us, although she hasn't yet explained it to me as to what it is. Our intended mode of transport is something called a Pelican apparently, which is kind of like a Toucan, she says. We'll see how that shapes up.

When we stop over along the way for a bite while heading for the Pelican Hub that's at the peripheries of the airport, she totally chomps into her masala dosa with gusto.

"Got used to the spicy cuisine as well I see," I comment rather inanely.

"Yup, I got well acquainted with all kinds of Indian food at the Beacon canteen, from Vada Pao with Mirchi on the side, to Udipi to Punjabi ..." she replies between mouthfuls.

I am so happy just to see her and talk to her, be with her. I'm not hungry at all, having gracelessly gorged on the meals they served in the flight. I just peck at the food in my plate, to hide my awkwardness.

She's such an amazing person. I've always admired her. I'm absolutely astounded by the strength of her conatus.

I know that Emmy has had a rough past, got bullied and kicked around a lot while growing up. But I can sure say that she had her own ways of bouncing back, always had a zest for life. The strengths she has gained along the way show in her making now.

We're done with the food, and are waiting for some filtered coffee, looking around at the landscape around and about the airport. There are portraits that are hung on the walls of the eatery showing various basaltic rock formations of the area from the past, of which only a sparse few remain in what we see out there today. The majority of the rocks are unfortunately long gone, eaten away by the encroachment of so-called civilization and the demands for materials that real estate makes.

"Do these remind you of Montana?" I ask her, pointing to the portraits.

She raises one eyebrow while slightly squinting the other eye, saying "yeah, maybe."

Not that the terrain or any geographic features are in common in any way, between Montana and the Deccan Trap, it's just that there is an element of old world magic in those pictures on the walls here. And from what she'd shared with me back when we were both in the Bay Area, I have come to understand that Montana has been touched by a similar brush of ancient magic. She knows that is what I mean.

"My hometown is Miles City," she says. "Have you ever been there?"

"No," I say. "Sure would like to visit someday." I've been to Idaho on a road trip once, but no further east, out thereabouts.

"We can go there together sometime," she says.

I'd sure like that. I hope my face is not looking like a monkey's flaming red ass. I've got an ecstatic thrill going on, on account of the invitation from her.

"My dad, his name is Buddy, he used to run a convenience store there," Emmy continues. "His father (and my grandfather) was German, a hearty Bavarian man. His mother (and my grandmother), was Ojibwa, native to that land. My dad had grown up modern Occidental in his thinking and world view, but one day the sagebrush and sandstone spoke to him and he felt the calling of his Native American roots. Ever since then, he felt more at home in the Fort Peck area and spent more time there than at Miles City. I used to run the store for him most of the time."

"What's special about Fort Peck?" I ask.

"For him, it's where the greater family is," she replies.

"The local white population in Miles City has been in good equilibrium with native folks by and large for quite a while now, but dad's back and forth links to Fort Peck and especially his trading partnerships in Wolf Point caused some sociological disruptions to the life in town and made him a target figure for the local disgruntled elements," she says in somber reflection. "I took a hit as well from that situation, and went through a rollercoaster life, both on a day to day basis in town as well as the milestones that shaped up in my life. I inherited my Teutonic appearance from my paternal grandfather's side of the family. Over time, I came to realize that it actually aggravated and further infuriated those people who resented my interracial background. I have suffered a lot of abuse, Vibe."

She really opens up to me now about her past. We had become very close during the early days, and had then drifted over time. But now the resumed connection is at a different level, and is much stronger, especially as I manage to shake off my awkwardness.

"My dad had a deep passion for mathematics," she says. "His geometric insights into practical real world applications were amazing. My mother Renata was Swedish by birth, of Okinawan lineage. She spent her life like a lioness in repose, languidly seeing the world through. No one around could touch her, except for Buddy, when she let him.

"The one thing I got from my mother's Ryukyu heritage is training in Karate," she finishes up this train of thought while smiling and nodding at the waiter for a coffee refill. "I made it to 4th Dan Black Belt," she says with pride.

"One common thread for my parents was the abstract academic realm," she further muses. "Neither of them had been a part of the establishment of the academia, but they were both feral scholars."

That strikes a strong chord for me; they are my kind of people. She knew that all along of course, and is probably why she never felt the spark with me. I remind her too much of her parents I guess, and that is usually a deal breaker on the romance front for most anybody.

I wish so much that it were otherwise though, for Emmy and me. But hey I know where it's at, I know the score; I'm good with the tango, as long as she gets back in the game with me for the Conch gigs.

When their daughter was born, Buddy and Renata chose to name her after the fabled mathematician Emmy Noether.

Our Emmy turned out to be very much a girl of the physical world though. The realm of mathematical abstractions was not for her.

"What were your passions while growing up?" I ask. It's funny we never had a chance to really know each other back in Cupertino even though we spent hours and even days together, building that igloo. Back then, Bonar was driving the agenda of course, and all we talked about was shop.

So now, we have a lot to catch up on.

"At the age of nineteen, I joined a biker gang, and was on the road for a while," she says, over the second dose of coffee. "The group dynamics of the gang didn't really suit me, so I then went solo but continued as a biker though, around and about Miles City, doing the terrain on my own along the rivers the Big, the Little Big, Yellowstone, and Powder. I did the Makoshika badlands through and through, moving around with collapsible modular living arrangements, camp gear, and bike."

It's amazing. At Cupertino back then, I had to cut through the bramble all the time, whenever I tried to get her to talk about herself. Now she is an open book.

"I had then hooked up with a so-called boyfriend, my first error in a series of trials that followed," she says. "He turned out to be a nasty piece of work. I had connected with him at a time when I was fragile in the extreme, and he traumatized me even further and left me in pieces."

This is a painful memory for her, she doesn't want to dig in too deep, and I can see that.

"I should have stayed a solo biker. Chuck, that was his name, was a really bad partnership," she says.

We're nearly done with our second round of coffee.

"But again," she continues, "as before, at some point I bounced back, and one day I dumped him by the side of the road," she winds down this thread, "having figured out that enough was enough."

Indeed, she found her way to an ascendant path, like a wildflower blooming out from dry cracked earth, and has been on top of the waves ever since. There are very few people whom I admire as much as her.

That was the time of life when she had picked up the thread that tied in somewhat with the one that her father had in mind, not mathematics directly, but cryptography. Her aptitude and instinct for domains of engineering started to come to the fore around this time.

The transit system drops us off at the Pelican hub. Two can fly with the Toucans, whereas the Pelican's beak as has been said, can hold more than its belly can. In the same spirit, the Pelican AAVs can hold a passenger payload of up to nine people, including the pilot.

"So what are you up to these days, here at Shahabad?" I ask her.

"Dealing with man-in-the-middle attacks, mostly," she smiles.

"Oh yeah, those can get nasty at Beacon I'm sure," I reply. "If I'm a guy, and a girl beacons to let me know that some bodily aspect of hers is tingly, I think I can do without the man in the middle."

She swats me on the head with a rolled up menu card. I guess I deserve that, my jokes suck. But hey, whatever, the coffee here is great.

We're ready to leave now.

"So tell me more about this problem, Vibe," she says as we are on our way out.

"Okay, I wish I could just put a finger on it, this glitch / breach issue, whatever it is," I say. "I'm going nuts, crunching this one."

"I'm intrigued too," she says. "There's no trace of a rogue message from the place and time you describe. Not at the core network, none at all, and none at the backhaul vertebrae or the subnets either."

Security is a major concern at Beacon, so it looks like she has already taken this matter quite seriously, just based off of the initial information I shared over phone, text, and email the past few days. I'm amazed that she has managed to execute such a comprehensive scan already. Well she is a hot shot in her line of work, why am I surprised?

A message in Beacon contexts signifies an event from an active customer. That is what she means by a rogue message.

The Beacon has a phenomenal A.I. Engine. The system sets default levels for people, and it is implicitly understood that beginners would give off red herring signals. Everyone's profile matures through trial and error, and gradually the accuracy improves with respect to how their signals are interpreted. This is great for the product, and as a consumer hook, since it adds a touch of thrill to the experience, but it further muddies the water for our investigations in this specific case, since we don't even know whether the glitch girl was a new or seasoned subscriber.

As of now, neither of us have a clue what to do next for the case, but we hope that ideas will crop up as we reach the Beacon back office.

It's our turn now to take a Pelican. So we park our head-scratching for now, and get aboard.

The Pelican pilot tells us that the freeway below that extends out of the Hyderabad airport into an outer ring road around the city used to allow speeds of 140 KMPH typically, up until a few decades ago. Now it is jam packed, almost bumper to bumper, and one can hardly do 30 KMPH or so, on an average. I sure am glad we are airborne.

The Pelicans are ingenious extensions of the Toucan concept. They are bigger and allow for up to eight passengers. On this trip, there are a couple of other travelers along with us, aside from the pilot.

We fly over the rush traffic. I have been hereabouts before, although it has been a very long time.

The Pelican's hull does not have transparent sections like how Joe's Dagger had. The bulk of the fuselage is some kind of an alloy material. But through a spyglass, I can briefly see signs for a place called Rajendranagar, and then for Gachibowli, way down there.

Emmy needs to execute a program and collect some computational data from Hyderabad Central University where some parts of that piece of work have been preprocessed by one of her collaborators. The Pelican does have a hop at the campus, which is why we chose this transit option. We park at the helipad that is nestled in the campus jungle. We enjoy the greenery and the sight of the dabchicks on the lake along the way, while walking over to the academic establishment.

She has a scheduled meeting at the department of MCIS, which stands for Mathematics, Computers, and Information Sciences, with a faculty member named Shardul "Hot Rod" Rathod, a classic car enthusiast apparently. They have been collaborating for a while now and are developing some subroutines together, from what she tells me. In particular, they've had a pending activity, to execute a concurrent interaction on a cryptography algorithm that needs to be done in-person and collocated, as required by the user experience component of the algorithm. So it works out well for her to make this stop here.

Shardul steps out into the lobby of the department building to greet us. His first name signifies *the one with a lion's mane*, but the fellow is almost bald, so much for being literal. He's a real affable chap though. They want me to be a spectator for their runtime activities, but I pass on that since I want to step out into the adjacent greenery. There is a touch of wilderness here that has managed to somehow survive the mad cramming of the surrounding city. I tell them I'll do my best to not get lost, although I must admit my sense of direction is rather abysmal in general.

I do manage to make it back, without having to place too many phone calls or hollers at passers-by. Meanwhile she is done with her work as well.

It is a fascinating experience, all in all.

We then fly on, headed towards Shahabad. This time the Pelican is filled almost to capacity. Along with us, there are five passengers who are headed for Gulbarga. Two of them are on a pilgrimage to Banda Nawaz Dargah, one lady is visiting family, and the last two are a husband and wife pair. The lattermost are lentil merchants.

The pilot does double duty and also performs the role of a tourist guide, regaling us with stories of the rock formations we are flying over, the Qutb Shahi dynasty times from long ago, and the more recent history of the city below.

We land at Shahabad, and take a cab ride for our destination. We go through a neighborhood that goes by the name of Ashoka Chowk, past Shahabad Fort. I marvel at the bastion of the fort, there is a good bit of history to this place. The cab then drops us off at walking distance to the Beacon office. Emmy needs to organize some formalities for me beforehand, for which she needs to place some calls, so we step into a mall adjacent to the office, in the interim.

I look around at the local crowd in the mall. An excited young kid is splashing his hands in the moat of one of the mall fountains and a man who is likely his dad is scolding him. Around and about are the usual families of shoppers.

"Okay, we're good to go." Emmy comes back from wherever she had headed off to for getting me clearance for initial access to the Beacon premises.

It is an interesting town, Shahabad. From the spillover of the IT industry in nearby Hyderabad, n^{th} harmonics have sprung up in nearby towns to meet demand and allow for growth, and this place is one such. A new form of civilization has erected itself on top of the carved out excavation sites of the stone quarries of the past. Something about the gradients in the terrain that have arisen for this reason, give it the feel of a temple town.

We walk along the innards of an overpass, under the shadows of the pedestrians who are walking up top.

As we approach the Beacon office, there are plenty of jokes on the innerwear components of the beacon ensemble amongst the conversations we hear in passing - the comedians have naturally accorded this technology the label 'The Internet of Thongs'. I'm sure glad I'm not the only one with rotten jokes.

There is a procedure at the front security desk of the Beacon office, where they jot down the serial numbers and other specs of any processor / screen based devices which a visitor brings into a jaded A4 sized register. I have my pocket conch which falls into the category of such devices, and Emmy laughs at me as I roll my eyes.

"Welcome to the Beacon Back Office," a melodious voice makes us turn our heads. A strikingly pretty woman extends out a handshake.

"My name is Valli Miriyala, and this is my colleague Nachiketa Mishra," she points to a friendly middle aged gentleman who is with her. "We handle Public Relations for this location, and it will be our pleasure to show you around the facilities and help you with your objectives here."

Nachiketa shakes my hand as well.

"Well now you're screwed, Vibe," Emmy says. "The PR department will run you through so many hoops, before you know it you'll be like a hamster in a circus wheel, no idea why you came here."

Valli mock punches her in the ribs.

"Don't worry about it Mr. Sangma," Nachiketa says to me. "We will make sure your needs are appropriately addressed. We have no interest in hindering anyone's activities unless there is a conflict with Beacon's Corporate Security. Further to that, our principal consideration is data sensitivity for our customer accounts. Emmy has shared with us the context of your visit here and we fully appreciate what you are doing, and also acknowledge that this will benefit Beacon to tighten up our security infrastructure if we do ascertain that we have gaps. That said though, client confidentiality is paramount. We will work with you as you traverse our organization for your objectives."

A young lad walks over and hangs loose, a bit of an urchin.

"*Arre* Faaltu, *ek chai le ke aa re* Sangma *Saheb ke liye*," Nachiketa shouts out at him.

He is sending the boy to go get a tea for me, calling him Faaltu while at it.

What a cruel world - Faaltu means redundant, or even useless. Possibly it is used as a term of endearment but still, it is a cruel term. I feel for the boy.

"I'll hand him over to you later, Nachi," Emmy says, waving a negative with her head at the lad. "Vibe, let's go get some more coffee at the cafeteria first. You can have the tea with Nachi and Valli some other time."

As we approach the cafeteria, the place is a heavy duty hubbub. I don't think I've been in the proximity of so many people in such a contained space ever. She navigates the place and grabs hold of her choice options like a pro.

"So what's the game plan?" I ask her.

"I need stronger access to the data loci," she says.

Data is a funny thing. Especially with the advent of qubits, things have changed so much. What used to be data centers in the past are now data loci. The towers of domain knowledge in these areas are each such formidable silos, whether it be storage, classification, access, you name it. Virtualization, coordinated stretching of storage along with the virtual LAN, all such kinds of things, the domains keep evolving. I am out of depth with most of this stuff.

"You're a Security honcho, aren't you? Don't tell me access is an issue, even for you?" I enquire.

"It's not that simple," she responds. "At Beacon as you know, we deal with rather sensitive personal information of our customers. Once you go through the paperwork and the walkthrough of the policies and procedures with Nachi and Valli, you'll start to see what I mean. We don't have exposed data anywhere accessible, as best as I know, so much for being a honcho. There are several layers of scrambling technology which one has to traverse through, and to be able to obtain useful information for the case you are chasing is a big deal."

This world we live in, it's such a sociological seesaw, swinging wildly between privacy and exhibitionism. I am a simple guy, can't really fathom it. Maybe I'm too simple in the head, who knows. Anyway, we've got a job to do."

"As for you," she says, "as far as access is concerned you are persona non grata. Don't even let out a hint that you have this case on your mind when talking to people here. I just told Nachiketa that you are a Security Auditor. Let me do the leg work for our actual goal. You just take in the atmosphere, and chill."

Emmy shunts me back to the PR department, and goes off on her quest. I set out to go be adrift on policy level for a while.

Ground Work

Hello, California again!

The trip to India was interesting in so many different ways. For one thing, it was a means of reconnecting with my roots. Although I didn't manage to go to my home state of Meghalaya this time around, but still the trip meant a lot for me.

It takes me a couple of days to shake off the jet lag.

The best part of the deal is that Emmy has understood the criticality of the matter, and is fully on board with this thing. That means a whole lot. With her tuned in, we have a good chance at cracking the code! Now I'm really pumped for this gig.

She calls me saying she will take some time off work and join me for this quest. I'm thrilled to say the least.

I spend a few days in a haze, puttering around in the igloo and stuff.

Finally it is the day of her arrival, and now it is my turn to receive her at LAX. I take a Greyhound to L.A. and reach the airport, to wait for her.

And there she is.

"Hey Vibe, hold this for a moment, will you please?" she says while handing me her laptop bag and returning the luggage cart with the other hand.

I feel the warm glow. Just her presence makes me ever so happy.

She has already freshened up in the lounge in the terminal and feels quite spry, so we head over by cab to the site of the incident, and Joe will meet us there. I had spoken with him earlier in the day, and he is all revved up.

We get out of the cab with a few blocks to go, and decide to walk the rest, to scope out the environs.

On Century Boulevard, there are the usual small time street peddlers, and moochers of various sorts. A strange kind of music is coming from somewhere, sounds like a mix of samba and African to my ears.

I can see the location now, the strip mall now so very familiar. As we make our way towards it, ahead of us there's a heavyset woman accompanied by a contrastingly wiry guy, they're both moving quite gracefully to the groove of the music. We amble along, carried by the same high.

It is weird how the media twists our perceptions. Back in Santa Cruz, I too have succumbed to this idea and perception that life is a chaotic mess in L.A. and the streets there are dangerous. Well there might be a kernel of truth to this, and this incident of Joe's which we're trying to chase down is no doubt a testimonial to it. But that said, life here seems to be getting along just fine, people at large don't seem to be worried or complaining. I guess the lesson here is that life needs to be viewed from many different lenses, for one to be able to appreciate it properly.

When we reach the site, I take some media shots for Emmy as well. Now that she is on board, she will need to plug into the subsequent iterations of Joe's Blow too.

Just then we see Joe walking over from a distance.

"That's a nice man you got there, Vibe. I think I'll like him," Emmy says. Well, there you go, I could have predicted that.

"I'm sure you will," I tell her.

"Hey, bouncy," Joe says, winking at Emmy.

"What's with the name calling?" she asks. She is grinning though, and doesn't seem to mind it.

He looks at me, radioing for a step-in. I think I understand what he is trying to say. I tell her about the whole context confusion that had arisen when I'd told him of her occupation being security, and his interpretation then of her job as that of a bouncer at parties.

"Well, now that we have that out of the way, you two can get properly acquainted. Aside from this gig and all this Beacon hoopla, you both have the wide open outdoors in common, so you can catch up on all that. Montaña, meet Mojave," I clinch the formal introduction.

We then settle into a rhythm and get right down to business, and start to dig into the locale for context regarding Joe's incident.

The glitch girl was totally relaxed and at home in this strip mall, and was able to walk off nonchalantly after shooting a man dead. Something that ties back to what made her feel enough at home here to be able to do so would always be there in the background and the atmosphere of this place. What we see and experience here now is bound to be connected to what the scene was back then when the incident occurred. We just need to lock in on the connecting patterns.

The strip mall vicinity is just as crazy this time around as it was the last time Joe and I were here. Right as we get close to the mall, we pass a young woman screaming her head off at someone, seems to be a breakup scene. It's not just hearts; people wear their entire lives out on their sleeves here.

It is a pell-mell situation, wherever we look. There are hordes of people everywhere, literally.

Thankfully, the walkway chunk right outside the Laundromat place is free for us to convene. After we are all caught up, Joe says that since we're at location, maybe he'll go hit a dunk joint now, following up on Heidi's lead.

That makes sense, and should add to the progress for Joe's Blow, so both Emmy and I exhort him to go do so.

The two of us go to a humble burger joint while waiting for him, and she teaches me the art of maximizing the lettuce and the tomato. Then we roam around the neighborhood for a while longer.

A short while later Joe joins us again, and recounts his experience at the dunk.

"When I went in there, I almost immediately regretted it," Joe says. "A bored looking woman was there, the kind of a person you'd never feel like talking to. Her name is Daithi, per what I heard someone passing by calling her. She asked me what I wanted."

"Well, what did you want?" Emmy teases him.

"I don't know," Joe says. "I just said *hit me up, Heidi sent me,* and showed her the card. Then I blanked out, I don't know what happened. Daithi, she is rank evil, I tell you. She just took me into her folds and everything went dark."

I look at him quizzically.

"On what basis are you saying that she is evil? How do you identify that?" Emmy asks.

"Hey Vibe, remember the thugs we met during our first site visit?" Joe asks me, and I nod. "And how about the fellow Munir from the Rogue Auto Collusion at the ledge on the Santa Monica Mountains, remember him?" I nod again. I remember the lope in all of them.

"Emmy, evil could be anywhere. Maybe where it is eerie quiet like they portray it in the movies, or even where there is a din or a stir like in this case what is in front of us," Joe says, pointing to a bit of a ruckus amongst car drivers stuck in the traffic and the cacophonic heckling of some of the bystanders.

"Evil is everywhere," he continues. "Just look around you, all over the world. One example you can see, is humans corrupting dog breeds to deliberately and systematically bring out aggressive behavior to the fore. In the end, the society ends up banning the breeds and trying to eliminate the bloodline. The dogs suffer, and the targets of the dog's aggression suffer. The mid and low level breeders and the dog lovers also undergo another kind of suffering, as they see their beloved dogs targeted. The evil top level breeders reel in their pleasure feed, laughing at the sufferers and further exhorting the hoodlums who misuse the dogs. You can see evil everywhere, anywhere. Here, let me capture a snapshot." Joe retracts a little flathead camera from his collar, and it pops out to the side of his ear and then launches a miniature drone lens that flies forward.

Ahead of us, the ruckus has built up into a bit more of a scene. A guy in a car is yelling at the driver of another car that is blocking his way. The man has to move over to the wrong lane, to pass by.

Later when he shows us the movie clip captured by his drone lens, we see the following:

The man who had been yelling is shown loping at the steering wheel, crazy angry and screaming. The driver of the other car that has stopped ahead of him is a frightened young girl. With her in the car is a woman, likely an aunt or maybe even her mother. The old woman gets down from the passenger side and walks with a pronounced limp that extends her lope, and crosses over to the other side of the street, the side now closer to the screaming guy since he is now in the wrong lane.

Meanwhile, the girl in the car in front is whimpering out of fear.

Seeing her, the man in the other car is now laughing evilly and then turns to the other side, and we can see his gaze meet that of the limping woman on the grocery store sidewalk. She has also been looking at the girl and has the exact same evil laugh going on.

The movie clip ends.

"Did you guys see that flash of recognition between the man and the old hag?" Joe asks us. "*That* is evil. They both relish the pain which others undergo, which in this case is the girl whimpering out of fear of a tyrannical elder woman who has most likely forced her to park illegally, so that the old hag can walk across to the grocery store with ease."

We walk across the block into a coffee house named The Bean.

"Hey!" Joe exclaims, like as though something struck him just now. "In that car scene, both the guy and the hag had that lope thing going on. That is it! This thing strikes the bad ones. Daithi at the dunk had it too. The lopers are by and large people who've gone over to the dark side, or are on their way."

"That sounds farfetched, man," I say. "This thing seems to be a disease that manifests itself physiologically. Linking it to a metaphysical root cause, hmm, I don't know."

The notion hangs in the air for a bit.

We arrive at the counter and place our orders, and settle in.

I think I'm swinging towards agreeing with him. Yes, this pattern of the loping gait is becoming more and more evident wherever we look, and the correlation is evident. The tow truck guys had this lope. Lanny Wayne is rank evil I can attest to that, and he's got it. The thugs we bumped into the last time had it.

"Okay so tell us more about what happened at the dunk," Emmy prods Joe after a while.

"The dunk starts out like how you would expect, pretty much," he replies. "I was stripped naked by the valet robot and whisked through a brisk shower and then swathed in towels and robe, and left waiting for a good time or so I thought, just like the usual rub and tug. But this thing is way different, man. They actually do things to your head, even the inside. I spewed out my whole life story to Daithi in there, damn. But it was cathartic, for sure."

Well, we've done some legwork so far that pointed to this Ennyk scene which we should be checking out, and Emmy is here now too. Probably our next step should be to look up some concert schedules. But first, we're hungry. Emmy is starting to feel the jet lag, so we should call it a day as early as we can.

So we head over to this place called Pablo's Grub House, where we sit down for dinner. It's a nice ambience all around.

"I like Inglewood," Emmy says. I see what she means. There is good life here.

"I'm with you," says Joe. "I come here all the time. It's not too far from where I live either."

We chew on the complimentary bread for a bit. I'm still not clear as to what our mission statement is, for this gig.

"I wonder where she is now," I say, rhetorically.

"Who are you talking about?" Emmy asks.

"I'm thinking of the glitch girl," I reply.

"Hmm," she responds.

Joe and Emmy get talking about the outdoor lifestyle, logistics of being out on the road, the best kind of camping gear etc., and share tips and tricks. I zone out a bit.

After a while, we hear a whirring sound, and a door opens up in the structure of the base of a fan-out pillar in the center of the establishment right next to where we are seated.

A booth juts out from inside the pillar and swivels in such a way as to allow the people seated on it to home in on us. The booth is built on an elevator device that has raised it from the underground area, to our level within the pillar. Also, in the same instant, wall dividers have emerged from the folds and have taken shape between us and the rest of the ground floor level customer booths. All the other patrons of the restaurant have been blocked off from us. The entry into this zone is now directly from the pantry, no other exit.

Facing us, on the swivel booth, there is a dark skinned oily faced man with too much gel in his hair, accompanied by two women.

The man seems to be in charge. The women both look manifestly degenerate, even debauched I would say. One looks like a squeezed out tramp and the other like a wasted harlot.

It's just us and them, real cozy, scary cozy.

"Damn it, I always do a thorough bug check when I'm in L.A., how did you guys find us?" asks Joe ruefully.

"You chased this thing buddy," the oily man says to Joe looking at him accusingly. "We heard you at that coffee shop earlier today, you know, The Bean. And what you caught on to and the correlations you started to arrive at, that triggers alarms for us."

As though on demand, his body starts to lope, in a very pronounced and exaggerated manner. Other associated physical attributes which we've noticed as a common feature amongst those with such a loping gait also show up even more pronounced on the man, unbelievably grotesque warts and boils. Then they recede back into his body, as though by means of the reversal of a magical spell. He can actually control it!

I'm shocked, and I see the same reaction from Joe and Emmy.

The man seems to indicate, that the fact that Joe was chasing the behavioral root cause for the loping and the associated ghastly symptoms is what has bothered them, and has led them to us.

"But your talk at The Bean is not all," the man with the oily face says. "You also spilled your own beans alongside of your nuts, at the dunk yesterday. Daithi duly reported the whole thing to us. You've got an ambitious goal. You punks are actually chasing one of us! Really, you think you can put your head in the lion's mouth and just walk away after that?"

"Let me first tell you who we are. I'm Randy," the man continues. "This is Pauline," he continues, pointing to the tramp. "And this is Wanda," throwing a sneer at the harlot.

They sidle up against us with a knife each, taking us on, one on one. Each of us is held, blade to the clavicle. Pauline's is like a machete. She is the one tagged to me, while Randy has a slim blade on Emmy, and Wanda has an oriental looking knife in her hand mock-affectionately wrung around Joe's neck.

We each experience different variations of lacerations, all to the surface of our skins. None of us dares to utter a sound, beyond some stifled gasps.

They then pull their blades back in, and start hooting and hollering. The three of us are grimacing in shock meanwhile.

Pauline is screaming obscenities at the waiter. They order for oodles of food. Wanda shouts out "Hey Chef, on the double, and keep it top quality."

In the meantime, they chow down on what we've already got on the table, also shoving morsels down our throats and lackadaisically mopping up the blood from our cuts.

I feel like I'm in some kind of an out of body experience, watching all this in morbid horror.

"We will let you proceed, just to see how good you are, really. If you actually get where you want to, then we'll see next what to do. Now beyond this, be a good boy and don't poke your nose into where it doesn't belong, okay?" Randy admonishes Joe. "You two keep an eye on him," he then says, looking at Emmy and me.

Abruptly, their booth swivels back and retracts back into the pillar, and Randy, Wanda, and Pauline are gone.

The waiter brings the food that they ordered, with a smiling face. We look at him in horror.

"It's all on the house fellas, enjoy," he says.

But none of us can eat. Terror has hold of us, and our entrails are way too clenched up. We slowly crawl our way out, grasping at whatever little straws of motor functioning that we are each able to call on and painfully execute.

Locate – Headed South

Hours pass, but there is no sign in sight, of the terror easing up for us. The night is sticky as syrup, and each passing moment hits us with extreme friction. I've never known time to drag along this slow.

We just can't shake off the dread from the Pablo's Grub House incident. We're at Joe's house now, all three of us, in a dazed and numb state, and it's not even aftershocks yet, it's the actual feeling of the incident itself that has not yet left us. It is still just as real as it was in that goddamn booth at the restaurant.

Joe actually had a stocked first aid kit at home, including tincture of benzoin which we've all had to apply to the cuts. It hurts like hell.

"Can you not do that?" Joe snaps at me.

"Do what?" I ask, having no idea what he is referring to.

"Don't pace back and forth like that, it is driving me nuts," he says.

"Buddy, I am just taking my turn. You were at it yourself, just a few moments ago," I reply.

He laughs sheepishly.

Yes our nerves are shot, for all of us. Emmy too is biting her nails.

"Who were those people?" Emmy asks Joe.

"I've never met them before either, but I could figure out who they represented, as soon as they showed up. I've come across references to Randy Logan in some prior contexts as well," Joe says. "He is a low life thug in town, on the cartel's muster roll."

"Logan is a strange name for a brown guy," I remark.

"No kidding, his real surname is Loganathan," Joe grimaces. I should have guessed.

"We will now have to watch our steps, these people keep watch on identified quarries for a good long time," Joe says further, as he bangs his fist on the table.

Wow, we're now marked targets for the cartel. I feel numb.

It is time to get a grip. "I am going to call in a favor," I say.

"Okay, elaborate?" Emmy inquires.

"My friend, Detective Pat Murphy of the LAPD, he will help us find our target, the glitch girl," I tell them. "We can't turn back now. Bravery is not my forte either, but my gut feel tells me we have a clearer path if we continue forward if we want to get ourselves out of this mess, than if we abort mission. Don't ask me why, but that is my gut feel. So let's buckle up, it's time to get our focus back to the task on hand."

"But I didn't want to engage law enforcement authorities," says Joe, "because I have been witness to criminal activities and I'd rather not get caught up in the establishment procedures on that account. I didn't want the hassle. That's why I came to you."

"Don't worry about it, that's an easy thing for me to work out with Pat," I reassure him.

What's not easy is for us to reclaim our nerves. We run through several pots of strong black coffee and in the end, we're even more shot up than we were before.

A few days go by, in like vein.

Also, before we meet up with Pat, more iterations of conch takes need to happen. We need to get a viable measure that will allow us to phrase our question right. Emmy's dual slides her way in as a bystander who walks into the Laundromat just before the shootout, and mine continues to do the moose thing.

Each take gives us further clues on the context, and we are hopefully inching closer towards tracking and homing in on the glitch girl.

Then we finally do head over to Pat Murphy's precinct.

"Hello Vibe! It's been a long time, how've you been?" Pat is effusive as always.

Pat says hello to Joe and Emmy, and introduces us to his team. The other detectives and the clerical staff are all very friendly since we're Pat's friends, and even the Precinct Captain waves at us as he walks by.

"Things are bad these days my friends," Pat tells us. "We try to do our job to the best of our ability, but law and order is becoming harder to maintain day by day. In such trying times I could not have asked for a better team though."

His colleagues beam happily at what he has said. They are a great team. In particular, his tech guy Jimmy Wang takes us under his wing.

Jimmy is quite a lark. He can talk, and keep on talking. His one overriding passion is his home city of Canton, China. Correspondingly, he has a bee in his bonnet concerning Hong Kong. He can go on and on about those two cities.

But he is sharp as a needle and has amazing sleuthing skills, and Pat says if anyone can get us to home plate, it is him.

"With network communications, it is all about Point of Presence," Jimmy grins at us. "I use statistical regression/correlation techniques to track points. I've got heat maps for pretty much anything that is on the internet."

We hang loose in the station for a bit, letting Jimmy do his thing.

In a while, I see Pat nodding his head pointing towards Jimmy, signaling me to walk over. I can't believe it, he has actually found her, and that too in a matter of minutes!

"She has used a scrambler technology on the Beacon feeds, a rather cunning pirate layer on top of the beacon," Jimmy says. "That is how she was able to negate the beacon signal whenever someone tried to lock in. I'm not sure how Joe cut through her scramble during the said incident, but that is a story for another day I guess. For now, we got her."

So we have a trace now on Heidi.

Alongside of it being a victory for Jimmy, it's a great win for the Conch as well. Sure took a while, but then I've never tracked anyone's spoor before. This detective work is virgin territory for me, and with this particular conch solution, we're seeing Real-Time Machine Learning in live action. I have pushed the Conch beyond its known limits with this one. Yes, I would rate this as the best conch gig to date. I'm learning as we go, too.

That said, what led us to the trace is a rather grim affair.

Here's the thing.

Of all the Beacon ensembles manufactured so far, there have been none that have been reported or found as lost.

There are two that have been tagged inactive and marked as having gone under the radar. One is female which is presumably the one Heidi has appropriated, and the other one is male. We got the trace on both, although our focus as of now is on the female one.

Prior to us coming here, Emmy had done a full scan on the entire customer base and did the analysis on usage, and based on a lateral flash of insight she zeroed in on these two, because the absence of any usage data on them triggered alert pings in her head.

The reason there was no inventory discrepancy found corresponding to the mysterious outfit the glitch girl wore that day, is because technically the outfit is not considered missing at all. The original subscriber is deceased and someone else, namely our glitch girl, is in possession of it now. For the two such outfits Emmy found in her scan, both the original customers are dead. Jimmy looks it up and confirms that both deaths are unsolved mysteries.

This gig is starting to acquire really macabre tinges now. Not that it should come as a surprise; we knew all along that we are dealing with cartel matters.

There was just a tiny blip of a Geospatial feed corresponding to the identified female outfit, which Jimmy is able to correlate for us based on Joe's description of the incident, and from that some subsequent traces as well. Presumably, the glitch girl figured out at some point that the clothing was 'hot' in the sense of traceability and neutralized it somehow, and so from then on the blip faded out, to the most part. But Jimmy is still able to track it further, by means of extrapolation techniques.

With fine tuning, what we manage to establish is that Heidi is on an evolving itinerary, currently zoned in around San Diego, but likely projecting further South towards Tijuana, and then likely headed out East.

The geo-locator trace has showed rapid movements in short durations, like she is hopping across towns for some reason. Pattern matching algorithms project an Eastward extension past Tijuana, for her route.

"Yes, it looks like we're heading South, into B.C.," says Joe excitedly, looking at the readings.

"I'm confused. I thought B.C. would mean we have to head north?" Emmy asks.

"B.C. here means Baja California," I clarify.

"Ah, OK I get it now," she grins. "I'm a Montana girl you know, my head is geared for the other direction, over to Canada."

"No worries, if it is only a matter of sorting out north and south, we're okay," I say. "But if we are heading into *Before the Common Era* then that would entail time travel. Who knows where this glitch girl is after all, maybe she is lost in time."

The joke falls flat, like how mine usually do, but out of it, I feel a strangeness that I'm unable to shake off. It's some kind of fore sense maybe, a taste of things to come kind of a thing.

All of a sudden it hits me, that the first time I had this feeling of doom, was just before crunching the first draft of this conch session. We're headed for something momentous, that much I can say.

"Here buddy, have a beer," Joe says to me. I must have been looking like a ghost. "It's just the devil winds from the Great Basin," he continues. "They do that to a guy's head sometimes. Trust me, I'm a Nevada guy, I understand it."

But that's not it. I know it's not, but I can't quite explain it to anybody.

Anyway, for now we need to close out the matter. It's going to be interesting, considering that none of us knows Spanish beyond the usual tourist phrases.

These days though, in B.C. you can get by for the most part with English, especially along the border.

In order to successfully rendezvous, we have to maintain continued Conch iterations, in order to be able to continue to tap into Jimmy Wang's extrapolations and map them to actual happenstance on the trail. This in turn means that we need a fully loaded and rigged up custom ride for the chase.

I suggest a simple roach coach since those things easily allow for Conch infrastructure to be set up, but Joe's mind is set on a souped up Zil tank as our Conch Mobile. He wants it flashy, as usual. I'm surprised Russia still exports those things though.

I mention that we've configured a roach before for the Conch, and the wave guide settings are familiar, so why not stick with what we know.

Emmy says, "Not a roach, let's rig up a Winnebago this time." According to her, it will be the right sized solution, not too small and not too big either.

Well, she is the engineer, and she is comfortable with calibrating the settings for a mid-sized ride. So I am okay to go with her suggestion.

"Oh come on, that's almost like a hillbilly ride, seriously?" Joe moans.

But she convinces us to go with her option, and the main factor is that we will have room to render conch takes in more sophisticated detail in the Winnebago as compared with a roach ride, which will be useful for this complex gig. She doesn't even consider the Zil as a serious option, much to Joe's chagrin.

Now where and how do we go about getting the right kind of van? The additional network and power supply units for what we want to do for this gig will not fit into a standard model RV. We need a *really* custom build.

Joe knows what to do of course, notwithstanding the fact that this is not the option he was rooting for. He is resourceful. He knows where custom motor homes are spun up. L.A. is his turf.

"You boys go get it, I have to draw it out in the meantime," says Emmy.

"Okay let's go line it up, Vibe," Joe says. He knows a place in Long Beach, just south of Compton to which the two of us are to head out for. Meanwhile, Emmy will go back to Joe's Manhattan Beach pad to work out the design.

Joe and I arrive at this place, where he says it can be rustled together right away. I am lost. I don't see any signs of RV / Motor Home related dealerships or any auto mall kind of stuff at all. This place is a hub for underground comics and graphics art. It is some kind of an epicenter for street culture, all kinds of ghetto scenes are represented in various media forms.

I step over for a bio break while Joe does his wheeling and dealing. "The restrooms are right over there," he points out for me. "Follow the corridor all the way right back when you're done. This is a cul de sac, I'll holler out at you when I see you."

As I walk along the corridor, I see various artworks depicted on the walls, reflecting the dominant comics and graphic novels of the day, progressing panel by panel. On my way back, it is the same corridor but somehow I get the feeling that the narratives in the artworks on the walls have changed a bit, within the timeframe of these few minutes. I can't quite put a finger on it but it is a very eerie feeling.

Anyway, how in the world does this place line up with our need for a custom Winnebago? I guess it's time for blind faith, hope Joe knows what he is doing.

He does. As we make our way out of there, he tells me that this comic shop strip is a front, behind which all kinds of deals are struck, for any given kind of business. Someone's got just the van lined up for us, set up with the necessary telematics and router configuration and everything.

The whole thing takes a couple of days to rig up.

By then, per the conch trace it is looking likely that Heidi will have crossed the border, and our rendezvous will definitely be in Mexico.

"Tijuana - it's been called the home for broken dreams," Emmy muses. "I guess some things are dreary around here for sure, especially the Maquila life of the workers in the assembly plants in neighboring areas. But overall, so much has been achieved from this region. I wonder why they called it such a harsh name."

"Nothing wrong with a bit of brokenness every now and then," I reply. "Some dreams might even be better off in fragments for all we know."

I myself have only a peripheral idea of what is broken here, what has healed, and what died and got born anew. It is generally understood though, that things have dramatically changed for Tijuana over the past Century.

Back then, the desolate side of this city was said to be quite evident, an ugly underbelly to the tourist carnival stuff. It is still there, but a whole lot more goes on around here these days, and the desolation of the previous Century is just a buried layer now.

In the past few generations, a generous serving of bright brains from the powers above took hold over Tijuana, and transformed the future, not only from a local angle but pretty much across the States of California, both sides of the border.

Indeed, the turnaround for the entire Coastal region had started from the South. Even the solutions for the water shortage problems from early last Century had come from here, in the form of efficient desalination techniques.

I'm definitely looking forward to crossing the border.

We don't spend much time in San Diego, beyond taking care of the gas and oil for the van, and the usual food, bio-break etc. Then we head straight on to San Ysidro.

Once we're in Mexico, we stop by the roadside and sit back for a bit, watching the slipstream and contrail patterns and formations in the sky that show up wherever there is a break in the cloud formations.

"Man, even in the sky the traffic just keeps growing. Still, I wish we had my Dagger here; it's so much smoother and faster. But wait, there's three of us, that wouldn't work," Joe says.

"Have you ever flown in a Pelican?" I ask him. He shakes his head, no.

"Come on, guys, let's enjoy the moment," Emmy says. "Why do you want to rush? Time is something that's in our hands for us to play with. This is going to be the trip of our lives. Savor these moments of anticipation as well."

She's right! For all the trepidations and forebodings I've had ever since we started out on this gig, I can't explain it, but I instinctively know that she is right.

Besides, even if we did have the option, how on earth are we going to be able to rig up a Pelican for Conch takes? The telematics wireless network requirements and the line of sight to the access points will drive us nuts, not to mention increased risk of further collisions, which we sure don't need. I shudder at the memory of the nausea from the last one.

The Winnebago is the right thing for the purpose. It does constrain us from getting a taste of the side roads and the inner city, but we will make do with the whiffs we get.

So we then drive on from Tijuana, aiming for Mexicali.

The surrounding environs of Tijuana are now quite densely forested, along the canyons. That used to not be the case till recently. A lot has changed for this region.

The interesting thing about the forestry here is that it has adapted very well to the scatterings of concrete and other such human traces that are in the vicinity.

We stop at Tecate, welcomed by a host of burgundy colored dragonflies.

"I've always liked their beer, and I'm glad the place itself has the same feel as their brew," says Joe.

We get off of the freeway, looking to get a further taste of some local atmosphere. We park in a meadow, by a side road and get down, stretching our legs.

There is a cottage nearby, where we can see a middle-aged lady hollering at a young lad, possibly her son, who is coming from further down the sidewalk. The youth seems to be bringing some soil on a wheelbarrow and is coming towards the cottage. It looks like she is telling him to stop dawdling and hurry up.

After taking in the local scenery a bit, we get back on the freeway, the Mexican Federal Highway 2, and duly go over to the brewery to get our one free beer each. You can't visit Tecate and not do that.

Then we drive up to a motel, since it is getting dark and is time to wind down. The plan had been to reach Mexicali today itself, but we didn't realize how much time the mobile conch sessions had consumed.

"What happened to your bivouac skills, Joe?" I rib him a bit. "Can't you rig us up out amongst the elements?"

"Ah heck, no, man. Not this time," he says. "I'm tired."

At the motel, Joe asks for three rooms. Emmy walks up and grabs him by the flank from his side, and says, "two will do."

Well, what can I say to that, except "okay then, toodle-oo!"

Joe is happy, he sweeps her along saying, "All right sweetheart, you're my bouncy castle."

I'm not sleepy at all, and now I get some time of my own, so I take out my hiking gear and go roam the greenery, aiming for a dirt road hike towards the Cuchama Mountain.

Santa Cruz is lusher than this place, but there is a different kind of green feel here that speaks to me. A solitary moth accompanies me along my trek for a while. I appreciate the company.

The border fence goes all the way up to the peak, gives me a strange feeling. Such arbitrariness on our part as humans, to say that this part of the mountain is mine and that side is yours. We started out living in caves, and ended up carving out countries. It stinks, why can't we all just get along and share the land? I'm sure a kick in our collective butt won't be long in coming.

In the morning as I step out for a walk, I see Emmy's silhouette, she is sitting on a deck chair that is still wet with the dew, being out in the open.

It is a crisp cut day.

"The earth is like the inside of my head," she says. "Those red purple and inky gray clouds you see, they are like my thoughts jostling to make their way out."

I see what she means.

In a moment it's all gone, the sun turns yellow and the morning has broken in full.

A genial man with a balding head and smiling face steps out of the motel and says "Buenos Días" to us, and we reciprocate the greeting. He tells us that he is a game developer. We execute the usual small talk for a bit, based on common VR topics, and then head back in for breakfast. Joe is up as well and joins us.

It is time to head on.

Truck Driver and Head Roadie

Ah ... Mexicali Blues. So many troubadours and balladeers over the years have sung songs of this place, the Capital city of B.C. I can feel it in my bones now that this trip is approaching a milestone. It definitely feels like a destination point. The spirits are guiding us in with semaphores. Bring it on, ye elements!

We park the van in an open area just off of La Chinesca and hail a local cab, since the roads in town will be tough to navigate with the van.

Joe tries some broken Spanish, to ask the cab driver what we should see in town. The guy speaks English so that makes it easy for us.

We head out to the vicinity of the Cathedral of Our Lady of Guadalupe, aiming to soak in the local colors for a bit. The people here look to be industrious and busy minded, for the most part. Enterprising street kids try to lure us towards the casinos, but none of us are the handle in the hand kind, and right now we've got bigger odds to chase anyway. We do want to just stay on the ground and chill for a while though, feeling the fatigue of the drive.

Once the feel of the long road we've been on is shaken off, we gear up for another run and head back to the Winnebago, to follow the next conch instruction.

We accordingly start out for a nearby Ennyk gig, as per the route guidance of the conch outtake.

The cartel apparently uses these roadshows as diversions for their undercover work. But in fact the bulk of the utility value the cartel derives from these shows is in the transit aspects, according to what Pat Murphy and Jimmy Wang had mentioned, at any rate.

The trucks that host the mobile concerts have a certain measure of artistic immunity accorded to them by the letter of the law, and without doubt the subculture that has evolved around their scene abuses that privilege. Therefore, border crossings for these trucks always end up being a pantomime situation, of officials and patrollers diligently dusting out those aspects of petty crime associated with those occupants that are not covered by the aforementioned immunity.

The petty crimes associated with the truck occupants are of course just small change for the cartel. The *real* benefit for them comes by means of the decoy function these trucks serve at the crossings. While the hullaballoo goes on with the truck, much riskier acts of smuggling, which carry much higher stakes, pass through blatantly via other cars on the side, amidst the noise and ruckus of the diversion.

Around here, all in all it's an interesting sociological pot of gumbo at the border crossing, the establishment dealing with the Ennyk folks amidst the huge volumes of the Maquiladora crowds, and of course the nefarious cartel thrown into the mix. Society is undergoing rapid transformations, even mutations, in this part of the world. Art forms have evolved around it. Personally, we didn't directly see any of these aspects when we crossed over yesterday at San Ysidro, though. It must be a time-bound thing, occurring only when an Ennyk truck crosses.

Well, here we are, approaching the venue. Some kids that are helping the inflow of traffic along the turns in the roads lead us on towards the large vehicle parking lot. Emmy, who's at the wheel of the Winnebago, brings us to rest.

The scheduled event is happening at a truck stop that is a part of the ever growing greater highway network. To be precise, it is in an extension lot, into which the truck stop would eventually expand. There are a few rough-in facilities that have been built for future rest area services, and the Ennyk organizers have ingeniously adopted those and set up shop on top.

This entire area is situated in the Silicon Border. This zone has seen so many ups and downs, both economically as well as ecologically. Politicians and social workers make and break their careers in this corridor. I can sense the ghosts here.

The secured yard is sparsely filled with shipping containers and sundry industrial equipment. Around and about the yard, is full-on jungle.

Inexplicably, we all get the feeling at the same time … that Heidi is here. No idea how or why, but we just know.

"Yes, she's here," we each exclaim, almost simultaneously.

As we're walking towards the audience area facing the stage, we marvel at the woods around us. What an incredible setting it is for a show.

"As a person of arboreal inclinations, I couldn't have asked for a better spot for the climax!" I tell Joe and Emmy. We know that the story is getting somewhere now.

It feels as though the filters in the sound system ensure that the sounds that reach the surrounding wilderness are duly processed for merge with the pre-existing sound waves in the woods, so that the jungle is a part of the trip, rather than an injured party. The towering cacti in vicinity certainly seem to be enjoying the music.

There is a band playing, as we arrive. The event overall is an offshoot of Baja Prog. Confusingly though, the main band that is supposed to be following shortly, is from Calexico, across the border.

The band on stage is just getting into a song as we reach the main audience pit. "This is called 'Ratchet and Pawl', and it's about how we move, folks," the guitar player introduces their number.

The opening bars carry enough mass to be able to rub shoulders with Higgs. Three drummers, with double bass drums each, rip roaring away.

Then, after a counterpoint pause, '*You and I ...*' ... the vocalist starts his yowl.

'*You and I, we traded our vows ...in a demilitarized, bonded warehouse ...*'

Right there and then, we see Bonar.

Incredibly, neither Emmy nor I feel surprised at all. It's all good. Everything is groovy, just like how it was when he first met us at Cupertino.

The song finishes, trailing off with a precision cymbal wash. The band takes a quick break.

Bonar is busy backstage and waves at us, shouting, "glad you made it," and signals us to sit back and enjoy the performance. He seems to be the head roadie for the band, based on how matters are getting orchestrated near the stage. The crew is following his instructions.

We couldn't have possibly heard his voice across the distance and over the public service announcements on the sound system, but both Emmy and I know what he said. Joe is just tagging along, dazed. This is his first run in with Bonar, after all.

"There she is!" Joe exclaims.

Yes, Heidi is here! Our tracers led us to the right place. And our instincts and senses once we got here, they were spot on. Who could have imagined, back a while ago, say when we went over to meet Marlon Jones at UCLA and were advised to tune into this genre of music that the glitch girl would actually turn up at an Ennyk gig we'd attend! Even I am now getting spooked by the Conch and its doings.

She is wearing a form fitting dress with Hungarian style patterns stitched on, strikingly beautiful. She sees us staring at her, while she is standing there in her blazing green, neoprene huarache sneakers, right next to the stage, which of course is a truck.

She then looks back intently at Joe and us in particular, and recognizes him. She is about to react in an unpredictable manner when Bonar fixes a gaze upon her and she relaxes. She is a mid-sized woman, slightly gaunt looking, there is a hint of almost infinite pain in that face.

She has a bearing of incredible grace. Her eyes have a tattered and frayed look, but that could be a deceptive first impression. There is fractal geometry there for sure, it could mean many things.

I am transfixed at her sight.

Something totally out of this world is happening here, all in all. Slowly I emerge from my frozen state.

Mesmerized, we just settle into the scene. After a while, we sit back in one of the adobe huts that have been rustled up at the edges of the enclosure, waiting for the hustle to wind down.

Finally, the show is getting near done. The band does the usual swagger with the last few songs, and then they wave goodnight.

The roadies, under Bonar's direction, pack up the gear and everything, and then they leave as well.

It's just us, the roadshow truck, and our Winnebago now. All the others have packed up and left for the night.

Bonar then rounds us up, and we just follow along quietly. There is a campground just off of where the truck is parked, where a fire is going strong.

No one is there, but somehow the fire is already ablaze.

I start to feel the uncanny element in a particularly pronounced way.

"Keep with me and stay focused, my friends," says Bonar, and we duly comply, like as though he is the pied piper.

We all reach the fireside.

Local clocks would probably tag the time as 3:00 A.M. or so. Everyone else has gone home, the band, the rest of the roadies, the audience, and all the hangers on. Only Joe, Emmy, Heidi, and I are here, along with Bonar.

We then see that there is one other person already there, a boy who has been in the shadows so far, but in the light of the fire we can see him clearly now.

"Folks, meet Tomaso Padilla," Bonar introduces him to us.

Tomaso is a bright young lad with a tousled head and grinning face. *"Como Esta?"* says the boy, smiling hugely at one and all. "Just call me Tommy."

My throat is quite parched, and as though right on cue, Tommy draws forward a refreshment trolley from behind him, and we all dig in.

A dog comes running up at us, while we are focused on the food and beverages.

"Memo, ¡Vete aquí!" Tommy says sharply. The dog settles down calmly at his side.

"That's my dog, Guillermo, I call him Memo," he tells us.

"Of course," I reply. He's a gigantic beast, very friendly.

"Memo is a mix of Italian Mastiff and Great Dane," says Bonar. "There is a farmer in the countryside nearby who breeds large dogs. This one was from an accidental litter; the farmer didn't want mongrels and gave them away to whoever was interested. For Tommy, it was a gift from heaven."

"Hey Tommy, are you from Tamaulipas?" Joe asks, and the kid shakes his head, no. He is a local lad.

"I was wondering because of your last name," Joe says further. "I know someone with the same name, and he had mentioned that the family has strong ties to specific geographical roots."

"Tommy's father was a sailor originally from somewhere in the region Horn of Africa, who somewhat mysteriously wandered this far inland," Bonar clarifies. "The people here opened their hearts to him and he became a darling of the locals. Tommy's mother fell in love with him head over heels, and he did likewise, for her. They lived a fabled life together, like the stuff people dream of. You know, true love. Then one day the sailor probably heard the seas calling out to him again, and disappeared from people's sight. Padilla is Tommy's mother's last name, although her family has been local here as well, for as far back as we know of. The boy finally settled on this surname, at a point in time where his father was confirmed decamped once and for all. The boy carries his father's torch of wanderlust, which is why I believe he is a key member of this group."

Meanwhile Heidi has been working away at the truck, watching us all.

"Hey Heidi, am I safe in your company? You know I'm scared of you near to death, no shame in admitting it," Joe says to her.

"She is a completely different person now," Bonar tells us. "A while back, I got some Peruvian ayahuasca, custom spiked specifically for her. Once she consumed that, her dark aura lightened up, and at the same time she 'lost the edge' so to speak, in the eyes of the cartel. Carlos, whom I'm sure you'll meet soon, then assigned her the job of driving this truck around, instead of whatever else she was doing before."

I don't have a good feeling about this side note of Bonar's about a guy whom we're likely to meet. It sounds ominous.

"Hey Bonar, tell them who I am, properly," Heidi shouts out at him, while eyeing me intently. I feel tingles up my spine.

Her demeanor is very much different from when we'd first seen her earlier in the night during the Ennyk gig. She looks all pumped up for the party now. Bring it on, whatever it is. This aligns better with what Joe described, and what her dual in the conch instance reflects as well, of course.

"Her real name is Connie, short for Concepcion," he obliges. "She has Yuma blood in her lineage. There is a story behind her name. Her parents dealt with some scary situations before and during her birth, health-wise and otherwise as well, and in order to ward off the evil spirits that were upon them, per their family customs they decided to pick a first name for the newborn that would be so embarrassing that people would laugh at the child just because of the name. This would reduce the chances of those of ill will inflicting her with further doses of the evil eye. So they named her Concepcion Asqueroso, which translates in English to Hideous Conception. The gringos corrupted the name Asqueroso to Hideoso, which is not even a proper Spanish word. She has the knack of turning things around to her advantage. So she then further morphed Hideoso into the nickname Heidi for herself, but usually goes by Connie amongst friends."

Well, I'll be darned, I am really intrigued. The cartel gangster side of hers hadn't really drawn me to her, but with *this* back story, she now has me hooked.

She has her sights on me too, I can see that. I'm still not able to walk up to her and have a conversation. The others are all mingling just fine.

"You drive that thing?" Emmy asks her. Connie nods.

"What does it run on?" continues Emmy.

"Diesel Ultra *Bajo Azufre,*" Connie replies.

"Ultra-low-sulfur diesel," Bonar translates, seeing Emmy's blank look.

"What are the powertrain and transmission specs?" the Engineer in Emmy is cranking it up.

The two girls then get into a zone.

"It's autonomous on the freeway. The autonomics gear is rigged up by Otto, it's a company from San Francisco," Connie is saying, while my attention drifts.

I'm scratching my head again; it's becoming a pesky habit. But something is yet to resolve, in all of this.

How did we end up coming here? This is a stretch for the Conch, well beyond fantastic. I feel there has been an external influence - also known as Bonar, in other words.

Call me obsessive and compulsive, but I always have to close out loose ends, as much as I can.

It really doesn't add up, as to how we got here.

The measures we got from the conch-takes on this gig were contingent on so many hyperbolic elements. It is highly unlikely that we were blessed with such a series of strokes of luck. There had to be an external intent and design behind it.

"Bonar, I'm guessing it was you who led us here actively, and the credit doesn't quite go to my sleuthing skills with the Conch?" I ask him.

"Well, it's a bit more involved than that," says Bonar. "I believe the time has come where I need to introduce myself properly to you all."

Oh boy, I can really feel it coming now. Something tells me that for a long time I'll bear the scars of denouement that I'll get from what is about to begin now.

The embers in the fire are about to die out, when suddenly and with no apparent intervention, the flames resurge with gusto.

"I am from another place, another time," Bonar continues. "I'm from far away and a long time out, far from this earth, and this day and age of yours."

I knew it.

He is an alien. He is a good and proper other world being. That's what he is saying.

I look around. Everyone got it. Incredibly, we are all quite at ease and totally okay with that. Possibly our beverages were 'custom spiked' as well, just like what he said he had done for Connie, to make us feel peaceful, but hey, I'm fine with that too.

"Well we're happy to have you here, my friend," I say. "Welcome to Planet Earth I guess, but don't tell me I'm the first person to be saying this to you, am I?"

"When I first landed on this planet, I set up base at the underwater canyons at Silfra, Iceland," Bonar smiles. "There was a lot of snorkeling and diving activity going on around me, and I would play pranks on the divers. I'd make sure they reached back to the surface safe though."

He grins. The alien is grinning!

The blood is rushing to my head. This person, our friend Bonar, is an alien!

Emmy and I still have the same kinship with him as we've had from our early Conch days though. I look across at her and I can see that she feels the same.

"What led you to connect with us, specifically?" Emmy asks. "I mean, with Vibe and me, back at Cupertino, the first time we met?"

"It was roughly time for me to head back to my home world," replies Bonar. "But I just couldn't bring myself to up and skedaddle, you know. Your world is infested with invaders right now, and so since your kind had played host to me, I wanted to acknowledge the salt I partook of, and decided to level the playing field before I leave. I was looking for people to whom I could bequeath some battle skills, and I figured, why not you guys? It just so happened."

Should we consider ourselves lucky that he picked us?

"But hang on, *invaders*? What are you talking about?" I ask him.

"Yes, unfortunately your world has an infestation problem," Bonar continues. "So I was wondering how I could help with that. Hence, as a thank you gesture for the good time I've spent here, I figured I'll boost up the powers of a few of you, so that you can fight this enemy."

"Are you saying we are the chosen ones?" I ask, half-jokingly.

"It was probably an impulse as to how and why I decided on you and Emmy," Bonar smiles, but he is totally serious. "The challenge though, was that you both are regular people, with personalities that have always been on straight paths. I was also looking for some down and dirty fighting skills."

"Hey, don't forget I'm a Black Belt in Karate," Emmy says. Bonar smiles at her.

"Yes, true," he says. "But fundamentally, you guys are regular, good people. That certainly has its role and place in the scheme of things, but further than that, for me to build this team I also needed someone who has seen the mean sides of the street and is nonetheless still reasonably immune to the manubrium bond. And sure enough, one fine day Joe walked into the game. He has gumption and takes on things with gusto, and although the invaders have infected Chariot and he is a product tester there, he has escaped their touch so far, which tells me he is fundamentally a good man. On the real dark side of the street, Connie has it covered since she's been there, actually lived there, while she too is basically a good person. There you go, I got my team. Tommy is the fifth element in this mix; he will be the bridge between us. He will make frequent connecting trips between where I am from, and back here to your world."

"Hold on, what do you mean by the manubrium bond? What is that?" Joe asks.

"I'll explain that," says Bonar, "but let me tell you more about your unwelcome guests first, since they're the ones inflicting it upon humans. These invaders are anaerobic entities who are executing questionable interventions on the earth biome. They are enslaving vulnerable humans by means of the manubrium bond, which, to cut a long story short, is a tool of biological warfare they are using against your kind. So, to thank you all for the hospitality, I decided to take a representative set from your kind along back with me, from where when you return, the trip will enhance you. It will give you superpowers so to speak, that will help fight the Orenk, which is my name for them. It will not be easy. You will have to be like snails on a razor's edge in this war. Make your way along slowly and surely, and don't let the blade cut into you."

Bonar then shows us a form factor based device he has, using which he has performed a lookup that identifies the invaders as near neighbors relatively speaking, originating from a few hundred light years or so away, but not exactly sure where. The device looks like a flattened out oscilloscope of some kind. When Bonar suppresses the white noise and the pink noise, the audio id of the invaders sounds like 'orenk', and that is why he gave them that name, from our perspective. They might be calling themselves whatever, but as named by Bonar, for our purposes they are the Orenk.

"I've been trying to locate their outpost but haven't yet been able to," he says. "It's probably on some Trojan asteroid. They certainly don't have the technology to influence the albedo or the spectral signature of the solar system as a whole in order to communicate back frequently and manage missives and dispatches, so they would have to be locally present at least to some extent. From the outpost, they would be enabling the escape velocity and facilitating the fly by for their return messages from the earth to their home base."

And he himself is an alien, coming from a much farther realm than our invaders. Will this ever sink in properly for us? I don't know. For now, it's all groovy.

"Why are they here?" asks Emmy, staring into the fire.

"Well," Bonar replies, "the same reason as what every invader has, to plunder. Maybe they want to convert the living beings in your biome into some form of extruded snack for themselves, I don't know for sure. Their interventions do seem to indicate that they are eliminating what would likely be toxins from their point of view, from you humans. They've already done much harm to your world."

"What do you mean?" Joe says in a startled tone.

"Emmy and Vibe, do you remember when we first met I told you that practically anything can be considered to be a machine, including an enterprise?" Bonar asks, and the two of us nod.

"The modus operandi of the Orenk seems to be to first gain control of the big machines on earth, namely the enterprises," he continues. "From there, they are devising ways to infect humans as well. One of the big machines they really want to take over is Beacon, and while I have been here, I have managed to thwart their insidious attempts, as a thank you gesture for having been a business partner. I'm not sure of their complete plan, but what has become evident so far, is cause enough to wage war."

"I'm ready for war," Joe says. Good man, he has steely resolve for sure. I'm glad he is on the team.

"I know, Joe," Bonar pats him on the shoulder. "One of the reasons you were on the radar for thugs like Randy, is because you did not get infected even though you were a product tester at Chariot. By the way, Chariot Inc. as a machine has succumbed to their machinations already.

The fact that you proved immune is an alert for them that you are a resilient kind of human, the sort they want to quell. This is also the reason why, as I mentioned earlier, I chose you to be a part of this team."

Things are unnerving in terms of what all Bonar is telling us, but we're getting knit together as a defense team, so that is good. I'm starting to see the pattern.

"Don't assume every visitor is an enemy though," Bonar cautions us. "For example, beings of my kind that are silicon based will have less contention with a carbon based biome, than those that are sulfur based such as the Orenk, who will have more grounds for conflict. They are the bad guys, they are local, in the sense that they are from *your* time so to speak, and have traveled space to come to your solar system with invasive intent. But I on the other hand, am a time traveler from the far future."

"How far out in the future are you from?" asks Joe.

"My proper time is about six billion years or so after your time," Bonar replies. "The Era I come from is known as Early-Chilled, which is a concept you will come to understand better once you get to know the Book of Light, all in good time."

Wow.

"So, you've traveled *that* far back in time, huh. Wouldn't it then be destructive on your part to interfere here in our contexts? Doesn't that trigger paradoxes, contradictions and all that?" Emmy enquires. She has the most scientific head among us. I'm the math guy.

"You'd think so, but over time, Chronology Protection has become a finely honed art, albeit a bit of a bootleg deal. But all in all there'll be no fallout, trust me," replies Bonar.

"Anyway, to focus on the situation your species is facing right now," he continues in an incidentally ominous tone, "let me explain to you why you are at risk and what you can do about it."

"So you want us to understand our weaknesses and disadvantages so that we can compensate and correct for them?" Connie asks.

"You got it, my dear. Spoken like a true fighter," Bonar smiles at her. "As a first step, you have to properly understand the concept of the smart machine, because that is where you are lagging behind. Back a century and a half or so ago, you guys built industry scale computers, or a bit earlier than that maybe - what you put together was basically processor, memory and storage, all boxed in willy-nilly. Then you added on some portability: mobile devices, wearable devices and so on. Then after a while you came up with IPv6 based technologies, and thought you were real cool and all."

Joe is meanwhile wolfing down various food items which seemingly appeared from out of nowhere, got cooked on the fire, and are now being presented to us on free floating plates. In the middle of breaking such dire news to us, Bonar is showing off his extra-terrestrial capabilities. What a dude.

"But we humans *are* cool," Joe says, between mouthfuls.

"Strong conviction and firm belief, with that you have won half the battle," Bonar smiles back. "Sure, you humans are on the right track, and your path does align with the way the cosmos works, but you've been kind of clumsy and clunky so far. You have to go back to the basics, like Quantum Field Theory and particle physics, and work your way back up to computing the hard way, don't just give boundaries to your machines in the easiest available shape. That's enough with the pizza box form-factors. Your problem right now is that these invaders are ahead of the curve in this matter, they know The Machine way better than you do. They are gaining control on all kinds of stuff here on your world."

"What all have they taken over?" Emmy asks.

"The Orenk are spreading their reach all over the earth," Bonar says. "For example, you know how bad the condition of the air is becoming in the big cities? Where do you think the new forms of pollution are coming from? Always be wary of air duct cleaning services, there's an example of something the Orenk have infiltrated. The actual cleaning is a good thing, not denying that, but it is best if you learn the skill and do it yourself. Also, be careful with respiro-filters that are in the market today that act as masks that accentuate facial features. It's a double whammy, on the one hand the pollution gets you from the outside, on the other the filters and masks infect you from the face in, and topple you over the dark edge."

All of us are just looking at him, transfixed. We can't really process what he is saying.

The world is under attack!

While we try to deal with this in our heads, he starts to fade out and in as we watch him.

"I have to shatter the illusion now. For that is what it is, after all," he says. "I do not really possess this corporeal shape which you all have associated with my identity. I have been influencing your senses to lead you to believe that this is who I am, just to keep it simple for you. Now the time has come, where we need to know each other better."

Slowly, we see a form emerging from the fade in/out, like as though from out of mist. Bonar's body is dissolving. From within, a liquid like and yet self-contained being, like a glass figurine that's still molten but mysteriously holding form, takes shape. A rough sense of a grasshopper like appearance, at least in parts, shows up.

The forest around us is quiet, as though it along with all the beings in there is keenly and intently tuned into this transformation. In my head there is a gentle rumble, and intricate rhythms being played out, maybe on an exotic instrument like an Oud, but I am guessing it is all in my mind providing random background music.

I am shocked senseless, and I'm sure Emmy is worse off than I am. She had a crush on him after all, once upon a time. That island prince personality, that debonair and charming friend of ours, has been an illusion all along. The real person is some kind of liquid glass thing, a being of a kind we could have never even imagined, let alone known.

The Trip

The form that has emerged from what we have known so far as our human friend Bonar is now no longer masked by human garb. A well and truly extraterrestrial being comes to the surface.

"Well then, are we still good to address you by the male pronoun?" Emmy asks. Wow, she's right there with the eight ball, even after this mind bending disclosure.

"You can, if you like," says Bonar the glass like being. "Let me use an analogy. You know how to peel bananas?" he further asks.

We all nod.

"Some bananas peel off better at the stalk end, whereas others schism optimally at the other end," he expounds, sounding just like a college professor. "Amongst you humans, there is a pattern. Males tend to prefer the former method of peeling, and females the latter. When going by this preference alone, both end up with a mix of correct and incorrect decisions over a series of peelings of bananas. Therefore the best option is to decide on a per banana basis based on multiple factors, not just the original slant. Given that people of my kind are billions of years ahead of you, it is natural that we are much closer to this state, than humankind is. You all have only just now started to understand the notion of gender fluidity, and have a long road ahead."

We are all completely boggled now.

"How are you even talking to us?" Joe asks. There *is* what looks to be a head to the body we are seeing, and what seem to be sense organs similar to ours, maybe even a mouth. But the words we are hearing are not necessarily aligned with movements of the said mouth.

"You just think and believe that I'm talking. Keep doing that and I'll modulate accordingly," he says. "I can convey in many ways. Manipulating sense perceptions is the means by which different cultures from various worlds communicate with each other," Bonar explains further.

It makes sense, come to think of it, pun intended. We tend to think that the five senses (and maybe the one other) that we carbon beings are bestowed with, are the only possible channels through which we can undergo life experiences. But what do we know really, of the bigger picture? Certainly, silicon is an element that is just as conducive in its own way to form life, and such beings would have a different portfolio of senses and perceptions.

I'm surprised I'm able to think this logically and coherently about it, though. What we're going through right now is definitely not a routine thing!

I'm sure Bonar is somehow helping make us feel at ease of course. Yes he is, and he knows that we have caught on, there's a rakish glint in the glass eye he is making at me. What a fellow.

I look around and realize that we are all inside Connie's truck now. I'm not sure how that happened, since my last clear sensory imprints were at the fireside. Well anyway, here we are now, in the truck. I look around at the Ennyk equipment. Indeed, there is enough room here to serve as a proper stage for a concert, I didn't get a proper gauge looking at it from the outside, but in here there's plenty of room.

"I know it will take you a while to get used to the *real* me, and that's okay. We've got some good times ahead of us. There will be plenty of opportunities to come to terms with the culture shock. I will now be taking you along for the trip of a lifetime." So saying Bonar makes a gesture, and the musical instruments all centrifuge out to the walls of the truck, packing themselves automatically into containers that mysteriously take shape there.

In the vast openness of an emptied truck, Bonar has us all hooked and transfixed. He walks around gazing at each of us straight in the eye, one by one. We've all been encased into snug fitting passenger seats that have appeared like magic.

"Am I going mad?" Emmy says musingly.

"You will all have to redefine your understanding of what sanity means," Bonar says with a smile. "Indeed, this is Catch-22, in action. You *will* fly, unless confirmed insane."

Meanwhile the transformation of the truck continues.

"Yes, we're going to pimp our ride now," says Bonar. "Hang tight, my friends."

The drummer's platform opens up, and from right below, some really exotic forge type equipment surfaces. There is a lathe and a tool for cutting metal, amongst other things, but they are not like anything you'd see anywhere else on Earth. There are wheels within wheels within this truck, in a metaphorical sense.

The same sort of transformation seems to be occurring, from under the smaller pedestals where the melodic instruments usually perch themselves.

"Good lord, Heidi," Joe exclaims, recovering from being shocked senseless and having finally found his voice, "What all do you cartel folks *do* with these trucks? You have an entire factory shop-floor worth of machining equipment in there, and I'm not even sure any longer that is what it is, any more!"

"You don't really want to know," she smiles mirthlessly.

"Well, you'll end up finding out more on that front, soon enough" says Bonar, "but this stuff is not the cartel business. This is my doing. I am preparing us for the journey."

Sure enough, the machinery is changing, right in front of our eyes, playing out an entire production process.

The hood strut unhooks, the engine metamorphoses. The exterior of the truck is transforming as well, in ways we just cannot keep up with. It is essentially converting into a spaceship!

But it still looks, feels, and basically *is* the same machine which served as the stage for the Ennyk gigs.

"We are now about to embark on a fateful journey. Let me tell you something about the Shifter," says Bonar. "The Shifter is a travel unit for one or two, or maybe up to a few people, as long as they are right within the perimeter of the unit. You can cover large distances, and achieve coverage that is effectively equivalent to FTL (Faster than Light) travel. And with skill, the travelers can traverse time as well."

"It's a fancy little dinghy," says Emmy. I sense that she is peeved at him on account of some Cupertino memories, and that is where her petty comment stems from.

"You're darn tootin' right dear, it *is* quite fancy," Bonar thumps a claw on a side panel that has taken shape in the truck/spaceship. He doesn't seem perturbed by her reaction. "The Shifter is born of something even more incredible, known as Guleil," he continues, "which as a matter of fact has been rediscovered just recently, speaking in terms of *my* time of origin. Guleil is a much bigger thing; it moves celestial scale masses in their entirety across large distances, and not just a small set of individuals and their payload like what we are doing here with your local Shifter terminus. The Shifter itself is a small piece that had been carved out of Guleil way back when, by the *others*. That had happened long ago once upon a time, speaking again in *my* home contexts, although from your perspective, that time too is in the far future."

Everyone is silent. I myself don't understand what he means by the *others*. Heck, I don't think I got any of what he said just now.

"It is confusing, I know. In this particular case," Bonar continues, "I have utilized an add-on and applied it to your local Shifter unit, which actually falls within the orbit of this Kuiper belt asteroid to which your kind has given the name Vostok. The purpose of the add-on is so that the Shifter trip can reach across out up to the Earth, and scoop up the payload. The add-on also ensures that we can handle slightly larger masses as we move. The plan now is to pull in this truck in its entirety along with me, including you people, plus Memo. This way, we can travel as a group with some food and other amenities for you all, which I have already arranged. I will operate the spherical segments for our Shifter trip, steradian by steradian, and in the meantime, I appreciate your company, and the pantry is at your service!"

We're all feeling groovy. Okay, Bonar, bring it on.

"So," Bonar continues, "this truck of ours is now a spaceship, or rather a Space/Time Cruiser, to be precise. It is a frontend device attached to your local Shifter Terminus. Let us now name it the **Klystron**. The Klystron will now cruise over to my home base coordinates, so enjoy the trip. As I mentioned to you, about a generation prior to mine, The Nomads re-instantiated Guleil after they discovered The Book of Light at the planet Agrahar in the Lego stellar system. With that planet being the headquarters, they then established the Visceral Empire, to which my world also now belongs. Everything that exists under the aegis of the Empire is known now as Visceral Reality, based on the name of the Empire. I look forward to welcoming you into Visceral Reality."

Sure Bonar, thank you.

The interior of the truck still shows some semblance of how it had looked earlier prior to this transformation, but gradually it is switching over to the look and feel of a long haul machine, a much longer haul, something interstellar, intergalactic even.

"There are some preliminaries we have to address first. We need documentation," he then says, while smoothly maneuvering Connie and me down the ramp, into an adobe hut that is right adjacent to the truck.

"Might as well grab your battle fatigues while at it, my dear," Bonar tells Connie.

Inside the hut, surprisingly, there is a sign for a stairwell, supposedly leading up. I could have sworn the hut was just one floor from the outside, at ground level. It had been hard to focus on the surroundings while at the campfire, but I definitely remember there were no multi-storied buildings. Connie seems to be hip with it and not bothered at all, and nudges me forward towards the door to the stairwell.

I open the door, lead her in, and follow along, appreciative of the curves.

"Bonar uses what he terms as symplectomorphisms, for journeys such as the one we are about to embark on," she tells me. "He is now using the same technique as a prerequisite step, to route the two of us to one of our alternate realities where the truck is not just at a truck-stop extension lot, but is docked into a yard door of an extended warehouse. We need to get long haul gear and also a Bill of Lading for the truck, so that he can use it as an anchor to swing us back here from the Shifter trip."

I am aware of Hamiltonian flows along symplectic manifolds, but I'm amazed that a cartel girl knows this concept, even given that it is an alien that has explained it to her. What am I thinking? This entire business is crazy. Anyway, I'll check with Bonar for the low down on this, when we get back.

When we are all the way up the stairs and step through a door, we find a whole network of logistics processing units - truck carriages, loading docks, and corridors leading to more buildings, both Quonset style simplexes as well as industrial complexes.

Again, it was just one humble little adobe hut next to where the truck was. What is all this? I'm flummoxed to the limit.

But Connie seems to know what needs to be done. She has been with Bonar for a while after all. She is able to walk the walk and talk the talk. I find her so attractive right now, and feel a raging torrent of desire.

The way she navigates maps on symplectic manifolds, what can I say, I am totally smitten. From what I gather, the truck is about to undertake a cosmic journey, and needs its papers in order. To get to those bill of lading papers, we need maps. This whole extended warehouse is set up for such like disbursals.

Reality has alternates apparently, I get it based on what she tells me, but it doesn't quite kick in, not really. It is not just the truck stop area, even the extended locale of the Ennyk gig near Mexicali in what we know of as our world, isn't like what we can see from out the windows here at all.

"This is just a taste of things to come," she says to me, grinning. "Bonar has a whole lot more in store for us!"

I must have been gaping at everything in that warehouse, like an awestruck greenhorn.

She then walks into a change room, and steps out in fatigues in a while.

"I usually dress in these while driving between gigs," she tells me. "They're primed for the tool work I do while on the road. I'm sure Bonar has set this one up with the right toolset for this other trip of his which he is now taking us along on, which was why he must have asked me to change into these."

We then get the Bill of Lading and other papers, and swing back down the stairs, walk out the door and connect back with Bonar et al.

Meanwhile the truck spaceship has been continuing with its metamorphosis.

From the forge that has emerged from under the pedestals of the musical instruments, various screens and consoles and other paraphernalia emerge.

"Ye all get ready now, for the thinning of the veil," says Bonar. "All this stuff that you see that is now the control apparatus for the Klystron, will hook onto the Vostok Shifter which I just told you about. The unimodal map technology of the Klystron uses dark energy to manipulate time. That is how we travel into the future, alongside of the spatial journey."

"What do you mean by unimodal maps?" I ask.

"Check out a 2003 paper by Avila, de Melo and Lyubovich," Bonar says. I never knew he is such a fellow nerd, look at him pulling out reference citations! "That paper is about a Century old, talking in terms of your proper time," he continues, "but it contains some seed ideas that reflect what I'm talking about. It deals with a wide class of dynamical systems, those arising from maps with parabolic shape, known as unimodal maps. If one chooses such a map by random, it will be either regular or stochastic. From that, a complete picture of such dynamical systems can be obtained."

Whoa, Dynamical Systems is actually a focus area of research at UCSC. That's probably why he mentioned it I guess, he knows I've worked in this area. I will have to go look it up in detail sometime, the paper that he mentions.

I didn't notice it while we were talking, but it is getting a bit hard to move around the ship, like as if we're trudging uphill or something. I am about to comment on it, when Bonar beats me to it.

"Yes, we will drag a bit like a parachute for a while," he says, "and then it will maybe feel a bit like you have windcheaters on during a storm, and then you might feel like you're climbing up and down the stairs even though you've been staying level all along, that's all."

We don't know what to make of all that, although it actually does start to feel like exactly what all he said just now. Then, it all eases up, and we relax.

"It is time," Bonar announces. "Let me now introduce you to the **brachistochrone**."

We become surrounded in augmented reality of a highly advanced order. Not the crude initial attempts we humans have made with our VR headsets and all that. This is *real* augmentation. The truck walls are screens now, showing us the outside as and when necessary. The insides of the truck, as well as what all is right outside, are all annotated in unbelievably ingenious ways. The truck / spaceship thing is moving forward in time, and on top of the augmented reality, the annotations are showing us the journey as we go. We are all individually as well as collectively cruising along a superhighway that feels like the East Australian Current in the oceans. The foundation of the highway is like a fishbone. A deep scale map of the cosmos shows up, with the fishbone legend leading us along the road ahead.

"That ... is the brachistrochrone," says Bonar proudly. "It has an interface that shows the backbone structure for the Klystron. Its gears align the Klystron with the surrounding vacuum polarization, and that is how we move."

Bonar is handling all the consoles and interfaces. He is made of some fluid glass like substance that is literally foreign to all our imaginations. He is part grasshopper like, and part like a basilisk lizard that can walk on water. This amazing human sized alien being is calmly at the helm, taking us along for a joyride.

"This is the mesh radio," he says, pointing to a specific device. "With it, I am communicating with the brachistochrone engine, and executing optimal control using the calculus of variations."

I start to see what he means. It is the principle of least action. He is applying the variational principle upon the Action of the Klystron, to obtain its equations of motion. It seems so simple, once he explains it.

We have commenced the journey!

"So we're really about to travel into the future?" Joe asks after a moment.

Overall, we're all cool with the situation. I feel in an objective way, an out-of-body experience kind of feeling, that there would typically have been something screamingly incredulous and preposterous about this situation, but in this loopy dreamy state we all are in, it's all good. There is a certain feeling of a significant change of state, like what one undergoes while skydiving or bungee jumping. But it's all good.

"Yes, big time! Excuse the cringe worthy pun, we *are* traversing through time. We are on our way already," Bonar acknowledges Joe's question.

"How much distance in space are we covering?" Emmy chips in.

"Well, it's quite a long distance actually, a few thousand light years. We would *have* to travel across space as well, once we move forward in time as far out as we're headed. We can't stay where we're at. At our destination point, your sun would have gone red giant long before, so the earth would be in the burn zone, pretty much, by then," Bonar says as a matter of fact.

We all mull on that a bit.

So then we're headed out for more than five billion years into the future, huh.

It was just a few days ago that I was a post doc at UCSC, working on a problem in dynamical systems with

Lanny, just another earth bound fellow. Then one fine day Joe popped in with this vexing problem which led us here ... but I guess it all started much earlier. I was in for this ride from way before, ever since Bonar connected with me and Emmy way back when.

Is this real? Who knows ... Or maybe a different way of asking the question would be, was what I was doing what was apparently a few days ago, real?

Anyway, here we are, on what Bonar calls a Shifter trip with an add-on layer, whatever that means.

"Buddy, can you give us a ten second elevator spiel, on how this whole thing is achieved?" I ask Bonar. We will need many summarizations, before it starts to feel real.

"Think of it in terms of Mach's principle to start with," he replies. "Once you accept an alternate accelerated frame of reference, you then become a more integral part of some n-body problem of which you were just a minor perturbation earlier. Then, by means of the Holographic Principle, you make the return trip when it is time to get back home."

Okay ... I'm groovy. I'm not sure I followed what he means, but I'm groovy.

The Klystron zooms and pans, out and in, from the truck stop where we were at, out to a scale where we can see all of Mexicali below us, and further on out to a stratospheric view of the earth, and then back in and out, then yet further out to an inside out view of the entire solar system, and then back to the truck stop. It does this a few times, and Bonar says "we are revving up, working up the RPM, so we're still pretty much right where we were back when we started, but getting a little bit further ahead in time."

Each time we zoom back down to the truck stop, we see further advancement into the future. Gradually, settlements start appearing on and near the Moon, Mars and the gas giant satellites, and keep gaining sophistication and advancement of civilization each time we zoom past. There is a thermometric scale in the Klystron that is measuring the surface temperature of the sun, which is gradually increasing.

"We're just warming up, my friends. As we go along, it gets considerably hotter than this," says Bonar. "It will be like each cell in your body reaches a thousand degrees Celsius, and then a million degrees, and then so large that it goes into the realm of absurdity, but you can't feel it since it is a system wide condition and you yourself are a part of it, courtesy of Klystron."

"Is this the beginning of hellfire now? Is *that* where we're going?" Joe asks.

"Well that depends on your state of mind," Bonar grins. "Heck, not really, you just relax and enjoy the ride, okay. Remember, even in your regular life, every cell in your body gets replaced once every seven earth years or so, with maybe a different formula for the brain cells, but the same principle. Aside from the consideration that the brain is handled separately along with the mapping of consciousness, what you are undergoing now is an extension of the same concept, not fundamentally different from your basic regeneration process, except that it is happening instantaneously, in the moment."

On the brachistochrone, we see ribs spawning in our wake, showing us that we are progressing forward. The screens and consoles that had emerged from the forge earlier get hooked on to a rib and the whole thing undergoes a bit of a stir and a shake, then they get unhooked and there is a repeat of the whole stir and shake routine with the next rib along the current of the superhighway.

With each rib hookup, we have a pit stop at a local reality, each time one step further out in the future as also coverage of distance. It is like a science fiction carnival, but unbelievably real. "It is real," says Bonar, as though he can read my mind! We want to engage with what is going on, but are forcibly flown through, allowing us just enough leeway to observe and barely satiate our fascination.

At a large scale the pan and zoom shows that the fishbone of the brachistochrone has a Möbius band structure.

Emmy is about to say something when Bonar cuts in, "You got it my dear, the Möbius twist is what brings you back when the journey is done. The journey is undertaken via symplectomorphisms."

Is Bonar telepathic? She hadn't even voiced her thought.

Also, I am now able to tie it back to the documentation Connie and I had collected prior to takeoff, back at the warehouse. It is symplectic indeed, this whole thing.

Suddenly, the sheer audacity of the situation we are in hits me with a thud. We're in a spaceship traveling to the future, with a possibly telepathic alien!

Are we there yet, at the point where paranoia should kick in?

It is okay. In a moment, it's all groovy again. Damn, Bonar has spiked us up good. Huh.

We seem to be approaching a station, where the consoles inform us that the next rib hookup is coming up.

This first proper stop of ours is a wild landscape. "This is roughly the 30th Century, in your local unit of measure for time," says Bonar.

But we are no longer in the Mexicali environs. It looks much more boreal, significantly more.

"Take your time to settle in, we will briefly peruse these surroundings in a while. Won't be staying too long though," he says further. "This is the border of Alaska and the Yukon, the land of fireweed. History is repeating here. Wilderness has reclaimed the land over the past few centuries, at least in the part where we have arrived. Alaska has the same geographic variation as has persisted over millennia, the arctic desert, the tundra, the steppes, and the woodlands where we are now."

"Before we go into the surroundings, I want to know more about what the Klystron does," Emmy says. Well, she is the engineer after all.

"Absolutely my dear," much of Bonar's bulk glows in response, presumably in joy. The parts of his body which we humans would broadly classify as silicon based equivalents of head, thorax and abdomen, show the glow. Pulses of the glow transmit through his limbs as well, which are connected to the thoracic region by muscle-equivalent body structure that controls the limbs.

"The universe is plotted out and charted by the background radiation and its temperature," he expounds. "In the past people used to set the local baseline for time by significant historical and cultural events such as the birth of a messiah. Over time, it got to be more convenient to work with Pressure / Temperature diagrams and localized Carnot cycles to track time (hmm something recursive about that). So I will not be citing your specific Century base-lined unit of measure any further.

"In this context, any give set of quantum fields (e.g. a person), has a corresponding set of places where it would fit, in the overall scheme of things. The Klystron (which is of course an extension of your local Shifter terminus) can then be used to achieve navigation to chosen destinations. In our case, we then do a boomerang fly-by to bring the traveling entity back to almost the original coordinates. The navigation consists of controlling the 'almost' part."

"Ah, that 'almost' is what took us from Mexico to North-West America on this swing of the pendulum," Emmy says.

"You got it," Bonar replies. "The reason for the swings is that we have adapted the trailer part of the truck into the Klystron, but the cab of the tractor unit is not the prime mover anymore since we have repurposed the engine as well to drive the brachistochrone which is in the trailer, so the tractor unit is basically hanging loose, free floating. As the Klystron moves us to where we are headed, the swing-along of the tractor unit makes us oscillate a bit. I actually like this arrangement, since it adds some variation and complexity, which keeps things interesting."

The brachistochrone shows that we are now at a place called Point Hope.

"Now it is time for us to quasi disembark, so to speak," says Bonar. "Just like the Gold Rush that you know of in your history, there is a q-carbon rush underway here at this point in time. It is the same kind of a pattern; prospectors, flashes in the pan, pay dirt, and sled dogs, lots of sled dogs. All that stuff is more inland than where we are stopping, though. Where we get off, we might see some whales possibly. In any case, we will not really be able to interact with matter here, so don't make any tourist plans. With radiation there may be some interaction, yes, be extra careful on that account."

"You mean to say we will be like ghosts here?" Connie asks.

"Something of that kind," Bonar replies.

We get out and about aiming to do some quasi sightseeing so to speak, using Bonar's term. We don't really meet any q-carbon prospectors, but are successful in whale sighting at any rate, so that is one thing to knock off the list.

We get back into the Klystron, and experience some further fluctuations that take us on a much smaller swing ride, just across the Aleutian Islands, and then our Space/Time cruiser stabilizes again.

"We'll have a few more hops before the ultimate takeoff," says Bonar after some time. "I wonder if we'll have glimpses of Titan this time around."

I'm not sure what he means by that.

The next stop is chirpy, it's a plastic jungle. People, domesticated beasts, and composite materials seem to be blending, threading, and weaving together, symplectic as a matter of fact, just like this journey.

"We're getting warmer in the klystron, and the cosmic background radiation is getting colder. We're now about a hundred thousand years or so in your local future," Bonar announces.

We don't stay here for too long though, no disembarking at all.

Then a dizzying array of almost innumerable such hops hit us before we can even blink, pretty much.

It gradually slows down, and Bonar says "I figured it best to cover off the rest of the warm-up in overdrive; the local sights are exciting since it is your solar system, yes I know, but the trip beyond is weightier in terms of purpose. You need to invest your time in the long haul portion of the trip."

Abruptly, it all becomes still and calm.

"Yes, we've revved up enough. Now, we traverse the throat of the wormhole," Bonar announces.

Like a maestro, he executes some controls on the brachistochrone, and we leave all that calmness behind us, as though we have shed a booster rocket payload. We are completely engulfed in a cosmic dance.

A whorl of Pomeranchuk trajectories zips in radially into my eyes from goodness knows where, and my ears are hearing some kind of incantations that sound like they span geological eras in terms of their time signatures. I feel fear. I can see that the others are undergoing similar scary experiences, at least the adults. Emmy, Joe, and Connie seem to be feeling the same kind of mix of exhilaration and panic as I am. Tommy and Memo on the other hand are having a blast. They're in a state of pure unadulterated joy, no element of panic for them.

I would have fainted, but Bonar is saying something to us, and I grip on to that.

"While you enjoy the sensory delights of this trip, do keep a bookmark on what is going on back home on earth," says Bonar. "The Orenk are hot on your tail and will inevitably abduct you soon as you return back home. They are autotrophs of a different kind than what you know of on earth. Although their life patterns seem to be similar to the thermoproteus anaerobes you have on earth in the sense that they metabolize through sulfur reduction, one salient difference to keep in mind is that they are probably larger in size unlike the terrestrial bacteria, or possibly their populations have evolved a collective form of consciousness that scales from a micro to a macro level. Furthermore, they might be autotrophic from their point of view, but as far as you're concerned, it is not a benign mechanism of the types that execute photosynthesis and nitrogen fixation like you are accustomed to. Your species, and as a matter of fact your entire biome, is a part of the soil they intend to 'fix'."

I barely heard what he said, given all the sensory fire hose inputs that the wormhole trip is throwing at me, although I do get that it is important. I hope my subconscious will retain it and recollect when needed. I believe the rest of the crew is positioned likewise.

I think Bonar is deliberately trying to keep us rooted in terrestrial thoughts. It probably helps us keep our moorings while undergoing a trip *this* outlandish.

"Also the ones who they have deployed to this outpost in your solar system, their scouts so to speak, seem to thrive in the comfort of darkness and deep cold, and will likely not get any nearer to you than the asteroid belt, but their human minions will get to you. You need to be ready for that," Bonar says further, when the zooming and whooshing machinations of the journey spare us a shot of breathing room. "In particular, Beacon is on their radar. I was instrumental in not letting the Orenk get their spores into the Beacon setup. They were able to infect a heck of a lot of corporate machinery on the earth, Chariot included. But the Beacon stumped them, courtesy of yours truly. They desperately wanted to control it too, since the Beacon technology, especially the jacket collar, is brilliantly suited for their nefarious purposes of forcing the manubrium bond on humans. This was why the cartel was on the case on behalf of the Orenk, and why Connie and Carlos stole those outfits."

Connie looks bemused at the mention. She makes it abundantly clear that she no longer identifies with that past of hers.

"But I couldn't intervene too much," continues Bonar, "on account of Chronology Protection. Then, time was up for me as well, and I had to head back home. So the best I can do now is to boost your juice so that you can continue the fight on behalf of your planet. That is to say, I will use the simple harmonic oscillations of this Klystron journey to enhance you, and give you some implicit superpowers. We'll see later how that plays out. For now just have fun, enjoy the experience."

I can't really process what he is saying. We have not had a chance at all to consolidate our senses. No time to even feel overwhelmed. We're traversing a wormhole, for goodness sake!

I just hang tight.

In a while, we again reach a calm phase of the journey.

"From here on, the tracks tell the story themselves," Bonar says in a tone that indicates the approach of something climactic. "I will now be preparing to finish my journey and head over to my next gig, whatever that might be."

Are we there already?

"Hey if you are getting off here, how are we going to get back?" Joe pipes up. He's quite the roadster. I'm amazed he is able to think straight.

"Don't worry about it," Bonar says. "I will program an auto-pilot return trip for you."

The Klystron sightscreen consoles, which are basically the transformed body panels of Connie's truck, show us the scenes from around and about, as we approach where Bonar is taking us to. Robot speakers glide around within the ship, telling us where we are, what time it is in the universe at the moment, and grounding us in the contexts we are moving through. It feels like a freight train ride indeed, where we are accompanied by wise people of the frontiers regaling us with stories as we go along the tracks.

Now we are all relaxed, and walk around the Klystron like kids at a science museum. Tommy and Memo in particular seem totally at home, of course.

One of the measures being tracked on a console is that of dipole anisotropy. Bonar catches me peering at it and explains, "That measure is for the Klystron itself, as it goes through the cosmic microwave background."

After a good while, we do seem to have arrived somewhere. A planet shows up ahead of us, and before we know it, we are hovering over the ground, a few kilometers up in the sky.

"Welcome to my home," Bonar says.

We are all amazed and awestruck, looking around. This fantastic place that is taking shape ahead of us, is Bonar's home world!

"Everything appears as though we are watching thermal images," I say. We are watching vistas of his world via the Klystron screens.

"As a matter of fact, your vision here *is* based on thermograms, so you are not off the mark," Bonar clarifies.

"Hope you have kept tabs on the bolometry," Emmy speaks up.

"My dear friend, considering that you've traveled through millions of degrees Kelvin, I'd say you might as well stop worrying about that. It's all good, trust me," grins Bonar the molten glass fellow.

"What's that to the side?" Connie asks, all alert and tuned up, pointing at a screen console wherein, as the zoom level increases the detail on the topography starts to show up. There are mountains that look to be sculpted in fantastic and amazing shapes. Can it be natural? I can't imagine there not being the conscious and active intent of an artist behind their formation!

"Those mountains are made of various naturally formed alloys, steel being most prevalent," says Bonar. "The metalloid staircase of the periodic table of elements is very important for our kind. Look it up some time, and you'll understand what I mean."

We all gaze with wonder at the sights. Most of what is on the ground will take time for us to adapt to. The sky at least is close to what we might call familiar, in the sense that it is blue. But the heady shade of tanzanite is not easy to come to terms with either. It is just a little less alien for our eyes than what is on the ground, relatively speaking. Like, seriously, mountains naturally made out of alloys? What geological processes could have led to that?

"Amongst those glorious mountains," Bonar continues, "nestled there in *that* valley, that's my jungle, where my kind live. You can call us the Kerole."

We gaze in fascination. Civic formations in the valley start to show up on the screens.

"My people have been around for a long while," he says. "The Kerole have been in existence for a few million c-years already and our immediately preceding evolutionary ancestors for several more millions of the same."

"What do you mean by c-year?" Emmy asks.

"I'll come back to that later, my dear," he replies. "But first, now that you all are here, I want to share the excitement of something that is tantamount to an upheaval of cosmic scale, in our way of life. In our time and place, in our reality, for generations, as children we have all grown up on legends of what goes by the name of Guleil. Up until a generation ago, it was just that, the stuff of legends. Just prior to when I was born, these legendary beings known as the Nomads discovered The Book of Light, and revived what turns out to be not just the stuff of fables and fantasy but is actually something very real! We now have Guleil!"

He looks around at us, we all show blank faces.

"Oh my, this will take time," he says. "I'm so glad I made this trip. According to some visionaries known as Mahabodhi Seekers, your kind, that is to say the human species from your solar system, has a deep connection with The Nomads. It is indeed my privilege to bring you folks on board."

Wow, now I'm amazed, awestruck. This guy from this here far-future land, looped his way back into the remote past, to our world and specifically to our time, for what purpose? What is humankind's relationship with what all he is saying? First we need to get to know Bonar better of course, before we can delve into all these wonders that he speaks of.

"Bonar, did you happen to visit our world for business or pleasure?" Emmy asks. This is getting weird now. All five of us humans on this trip, our minds are getting interconnected. The same thoughts are striking us, at the same time. I look in Memo's eyes, and he is in lockstep too!

"Yeah buddy, tell us," I continue her question. "Was your trip intentional, or did you happen to hit our light cones in a most random way? And are you now giving us a joy ride to *your* time, as a goodbye gesture for us?"

He grins back. We sense that we won't get any immediate answers. The picture will acquire shape as we go.

Bonar has graciously molded a face for himself with eyes, ears, et cetera, basically for our benefit, so he hasn't appeared all *that* alien to us even up till this point. We are now looking out at the rest of his folks and their body structures vary widely, and don't often align with how we expect living beings to look like. Some of them are highly ornate and look to be done up like Mandarin ducks or something, whereas others are sparsely expressed and minimalist. In between, there seems to be a large spectrum of personality types. It is hard for us humans to grasp, as to whether this is one species or an entire sub-biome, we can't really tell.

Connie comes over to the back of the truck and walks up close to me. There is a key with an image of a skull that dangles from a clasp on her belt buckle.

"What's that?" I ask her, pointing to the key.

"Well," she smiles. "That is the key to your head."

"I don't think so," I parry. "My mind is open, has no lock."

"Be careful," she says. "If the mind is too open, the brain might spill out."

It is uncanny. Here we are in her souped up truck cruiser, zipping through space and time, who knows how many billions of years out into the future, how many light-years away from the Earth, and we're all totally with it, hip with it, no one feels any incongruity. We're even able to undertake small talk!

"You see those sand hills over there?" Bonar asks us, pointing at one of the Klystron screen consoles, which is zoomed into the area on the ground that he is referring to. "You can think of them like umbilical cords for our people, except that we keep returning and connecting back to them over the course of our lives. We get special nourishment from there, on occasions of growth spurts. We literally live off the land; that is how we are made. Here we are born, grow, travel return trips back to here, and die."

Yes, we can see youngsters of Bonar's kind rolling about and frolicking in the sands. They look like throbbing lumps of glass, jumping around like how otters do on Earth. Size wise as well, the kids would be comparable to how marine mammal cubs are on the earth, but they have wings growing on their backs. Other than the jumping aspect, they don't have anything else in common with the otters though. They look very different from any earth based life form we are aware of.

"Do your kids go to school?" Joe asks.

"Well, you will have to extrapolate significantly from that concept which you are familiar with," Bonar replies. "The trips we make across time via the Shifter automatically address that need, especially when accompanied by a mentor. Now, Guleil is changing everything of course, it will all be much grander in scale now."

We continue watching, in fascination.

The Kerole are able to adjust their shape while in motion. The adults are bluish-green beings that are reminiscent of glass figurines that are still in the final stage of remaining molten, just before acquiring solid state. Their organs can be seen through the translucence of their bodies, and it is not strange at all, rather mesmerizing in fact. For simplicity's sake, we could think of them as dragonfly or grasshopper like beings with a touch of the basilisk lizard thrown in, maybe even an otter touch, overall some kind of mix of insect and reptile and mammal form. But not really, we do have to shrug off our anthropomorphic lenses to see them properly, or else we will keep mentally adding various animal references, which would more often than not end up being quite off base. They are human sized at any rate, give or take an order of magnitude either side.

Some Kerole are giant beings, some our size, and some fairly small.

"I'm amazed at how the patterns of life are so similar even this far out, billions of years from our time," says Emmy, looking avidly at the Kerole.

"Some things are fundamental in the cosmos, such as the fine structure so-called 'constant', and the Euler identity," Bonar replies. "Life always aligns with and conforms to such foundational elements, at any stage of the evolution of the universe."

I'm still focused on the Kerole kids, watching them execute various activities that look quite exotic, at least to me. "Some patterns are similar, yes. Some are strikingly different," I say.

"Naturally, that is so," Bonar smiles. "What you are seeing here is, our children are figuring out how to tap into our fundamental nature. You know how semiconductors work? In some conditions they conduct electricity, and in other conditions they don't. Our kind shows that pattern, in the way we live. With us it is not just electricity of course. The junction diode metaphor applies to us on so many levels."

I can indeed see the pattern of charge carriers in a crystal lattice, being applicable to the way these children are growing up. It is awe inspiring.

Bonar seems to be intently working on the Klystron's mechanism in the meanwhile.

"Now I will try to work out some motor action on this end," he says. "Before we part ways, let me see if I can show you people what I was talking about earlier. It will be wonderful if you can see what is happening with Guleil, at the outer reaches of my stellar system."

He does some lookups and checks on the brachistochrone, and seems satisfied.

"Yes, it is feasible," he says, beaming with joy. "I was testing the elasticity of the Klystron in terms of being able to swing us across to the outer reaches of my stellar system, and then back here for your return trip. In your solar system, the Shifter Terminus happens to be in the Kuiper Belt, but here for us it is more interior. The Shifter location varies by stellar system. Each system has its own configuration."

So, we will now be able to go see this thing called Guleil.

"I will take you now for a scenic detour to show the initial setup of a Guleil hub," Bonar continues, confirming my understanding. "Mind you, this is as yet an experimental technology. The Nomads have founded the Empire just a generation ago, and our stellar system was one of the early participants."

We start to move, accelerating quite rapidly. Bonar's home planet dwindles away to a tiny dot. The Klystron screens show us breathtaking views of some of the celestial bodies in his stellar system, as we fly past. We pass by a few other planets, including some gar giants.

We're slowly starting to understand what Guleil means. It is a means by which entire populations of sentient beings can travel really far, out across the universe, much farther than even Hollywood can imagine. Instead of using ships, they use dwarf planets to travel.

"Bonar, do you know if the sentient beings in *our* solar system ever evolved to the point of being able to participate in Guleil?" Emmy asks.

"I'm afraid your stellar system was born in the wrong time," Bonar replies. "Your sun went red giant long before even the very early forms of Guleil were instantiated. I believe there will be some proto-dreams to come in your far future at some point, where mankind will participate in some Guleil type attempts with the help of beings known as pipers, who will be some very early reflections of what Pivots are to be for the universe, much later. But that whole attempt for your solar system would only be a dream of an attempt."

That is brutal. Does that mean our kind never really makes it across the wider cosmos, journeys across distances of thousands and even millions of light years, which this Guleil seems to be facilitating? Are we destined to die out like frogs local to our own little well?

Bonar seems to have sensed that feeling of tragedy we are all experiencing, as we process what he has told us just now.

"Of course, it is quite conceivable that some stowaway human genomes might have sailed past the collective boundaries of all the nearby helio-systems your kind does reach, by means of the space technologies you do manage to achieve, within your sun's lifespan," he says in a consoling tone. "Some of those genomes might well have borne humans in such adopted new homes for your kind, whose descendants might well have continued to evolve into the times I myself am from, and could then have participated in Guleil too at some point, from some new home planet. In my proper time, I myself have never come across any such beings whom I could classify as humans of the likes of you, but who knows, it is a significantly extant cosmos after all, and your immediate kind might well be around somewhere. Also, there are sure to be plenty of Visceral hitchhikers like yourselves, brought over via the Shifter. So don't worry, you won't be all that lonely."

While we have been talking, the Klystron has cut through the blackness of space, and we have reached a point from where we can see an Arch-Pivot Station, and a target minor planet. We will now see Guleil in action!

The workings of Guleil are explained in The Book of Light, which The Nomads discovered just a generation or so prior to Bonar's time.

Guleil is a mechanism to facilitate 'FTL Equivalent' (Faster than Light Equivalent) travel, across Space/Time.

The equivalence is quote/unquote on account of the consideration that wormholes connect space-like separated points, exploit non-trivial topologies, and use exotic matter to get across, get around, get by, and get wherever. Therefore the speed of light doesn't really apply to it as a threshold. Guleil allows you to travel universe-scale distances, and also across time in principle. Travel through time would have to be done while still maintaining the integrity of closed time-like curves, and making that happen for an entire planet can get very hairy. Hence it remains an in-principle possibility, to the most part.

A typical space propulsion technology we earthlings are accustomed to, even in concept, would have payload capacity of a few people, maybe a few hundred if it is part of a starship fleet. Guleil on the other hand, moves dwarf planets around. It can carry entire populations of sentient beings.

Right in front of our eyes, poof … a minor planet disappears, and another one reappears in its place.

We all stay in stunned silence just absorbing and processing what we just saw, while Bonar flies us back to his home planet.

Wow, that was amazing. We're back now, hovering above Bonar's planet, where he will soon exit using the Shifter unit there.

What is next for us now? Bonar lays it out for us.

The four of us adults have approached the phase in life where we need set patterns in life, and time to head back home and settle down. But Tommy is young, and can do some backpacking around the cosmos for a while. So Bonar will take Tommy with him and set him off for his future trips as and when he is ready.

For the multiple trips Tommy goes on, he will be ensconced in a specially constructed sphere which helps maintain his metabolism through all the transitions. He is thus the boy in the bubble.

"He has many exciting trips ahead of him, and in preparation for that, he is now in camera, and no longer with you now," says Bonar. "While he journeys thus among Visceral worlds, to you he will be the deaf, dumb, and blind kid."

"So, will he ever come back to the earth, and be one of us again?" Connie asks. "What about Memo?"

"Memo will return to the earth with you," says Bonar. "In fact, you hit the nail on the head. The dog will be the boy's link back to your world, and for the sake of the dog, the boy will visit you at appropriate moments. In the meantime, Memo will consider Connie to be his primary human companion, in the absence of Tommy."

"I will modulate two sets of knowledge nuggets on to each of Tommy's return trips, which you will have to decrypt and act on each time," says Bonar. "One set would be controls for Tommy's trips, which will also help you get to know The Book of Light. The other set will be for you to use in your own world, to fight enemies like the Orenk."

So, Emmy and I need to brush up on our math and other necessary skills and knowledge when the time comes. On the one hand, we need to be able to execute the space-time traffic control for Tommy's oscillations, when we are called upon and that would be mostly with Emmy and me. On the other hand, we need to interpret the second sets of nuggets to obtain solutions for the problems of our world, and mainly it will be Connie and Joe who will deal with the practical matters pertaining to this set. They will have to influence statesmen, lobbies, and corporate interests to fix up the house. This seems to be the long haul picture, our future.

"All that knowledge stuff will be on top of the powers that you will gain. But you need to hide your powers," says Bonar, "because the Orenk should think of you as regular humans who have maybe come to know too much somehow, and hence at most a mild threat. But that should be a bargaining strength for you, use it to join their ranks. They should feel comfortable enough in their state of power, and believe that you are not a real threat. And in the background, for all the fixes and solutions you provide to your world, let others take the credit, the money and power, and all that comes with it. You people will have to lie low. A fat lot of good it will do to you if you are momentarily rich and powerful, and then get taken down by the Orenk since you've blown your cover too early."

We all nod. We see the wisdom in that. None of us are really into that rat race game, anyway. Joe is already rich, but has made it there based on solid merit and clean deals. There is no disparity in the interactions amongst us on that account, as to who is loaded how much. All of us are sensibly well grounded.

Our Shifter powers will comprehensively prevent the hold of the manubrium bond for us, whatever that means, without the Orenk getting to know about it.

"Bonar, so you are a genie now," Connie says, "granting us superpowers."

"Sure thing, Connie, that analogy works," says Bonar. "It does come with the rider though that if you take me up on it, you will gradually lose connection with your prior selves, and per the black hole thermodynamics of the trip you have taken, it is irreversible. Whoever chooses not to take the powers, will be able to retain stronger links to prior contexts. It is all in the way chronology protection pans out."

"What do you mean exactly?" I ask him.

"Let's assume some of you keep the Visceral link and the rest break it, labeled respectively as Set A and Set B," says Bonar. "As you go forward in life, it is highly unlikely, in fact infinitely improbable, that the Set A folks will be able to retain any close connections with anyone else back on earth, not even with the Set B folks even though the latter took the same journey. The Set B folks on the other hand will be able to reconnect as they desire with the rest of the earthlings, since the imprint of this journey will effectively be rolled back from their identities. But Set A will stand alone."

So, those of us who want the powers and hence will have to keep the Visceral link, will only have each other to connect with. Gradually, we will find other Visceral connections each, maybe. But it will be lonely at the start.

"Make up your minds comprehensively, my friends," says Bonar. "You only go to the well once."

No surprise though, we all opt in, to be a part of Set A. No one is in Set B. What is the point in going back to our old lives, if the world that we know is going to be done in by the Orenk anyway? To fight them and save the world for our kind, we need the powers.

So now, we have to choose the powers we need.

I know mine. I want to internalize the Conch. I want to know the way, the answers, without having to carry the clunky trappings of the machine.

"I want to be able to connect asymptotic dots on my own, Bonar," I ask. "I want to take the gloves off, and be able to measure directly, with my mind knuckles. No igloo, no pocket conch, no conch mobile, just my mind."

He smiles like as though he already knew it. He probably did.

"I want the ability to regenerate from protoplasm," says Emmy. She is asking for a shade of immortality is how I understand it.

"Well Emmy, now that you are on a Shifter trip, your identity is already mapped Viscerally, and in effect can be regenerated on demand. So you already have that wish granted to you. This holds for all of you as a matter of fact," says Bonar.

I'm dumbfounded. Is that really so?

"That of course is capped by the time frame of whatever turns out to be the mechanism of natural death for each of you," he continues. "The Visceral regeneration goes only that far and no further." That makes sense.

"Okay then. I want to be able to walk on water and not get burned by fire," Emmy adds to her list.

"I want to win every battle I'm in," says Joe, simple and to the point.

"Have you ever heard of King Vikram's tales, Joe?" Bonar asks. "In every episode, Vikram cracks the code each time and wins against earthly as well as supernatural enemies, but he is then inevitably saddled with yet another battle. You can have that wish granted if you want, but it comes with strings attached." Joe grimaces, trying to figure out what that means.

"I want to get elemental," says Connie. "I want to be able to flow from moment to moment and point to point with no hindrance, either as my usual physical self and body if that works and in which case no action needed, or as a generated entity from whatever elements I am in the presence of that will allow me to keep with the flow. Nothing should be able to stop me when I want to flow. For example, if I am at a mountain ledge where there is a landslide underway, I want to be able to turn into a big and badass boulder myself and just keep rolling, and turn back again to my human body, when I hit the plains and the rocks stop sliding."

She sure has a vivid imagination.

Bonar just grins, and says, "Let me access some power source vaults via the brachistochrone, to see what I can do for you all."

All fine and dandy, but the chronology protection will ensure that no one else here can sense any of that. We are going to be truly incognito and fully undercover. Only Closed Time-like Curves (CTCs) are permissible for any world lines that we traverse along, which forbids information leaks across the Cauchy Horizon. This means that any fellow human beings with whom we share our proper time, cannot observe or become aware of any Visceral boosts we get empowered with, since there are Cauchy Horizons between us and Visceral Reality, which only we will be able to transcend because of our Shifter link.

If we can understand the subtleties of the light cone tilts of our trajectories then we can take slight advantage of the holographic principle here and there.

Even amongst the four us, if any of us wants children, Bonar says it is beyond his abilities to predict and plan for the outcome, as to whether the children will get the Visceral connection from us or not. He says Tommy will grow into a wise ol' Visceral wizard and should be able to help clarify such finer points of our lives, later on down the line. His connection to us will be because of Memo. He does have a cordial equation with Connie as well but that is still at an acquaintance level. The only thing that will periodically draw him back to reconnect with us will be Memo.

Another way to grow our cadres will be to trigger a Shifter trip ourselves, but that requires much knowledge. One day, hopefully we'll get there.

"Vibe, you infuriating fellow, I thought I had it all worked out, but you found a way to hassle me with this genie task," Bonar says to me. "You know how to dig out intractable problems, don't you? Once a nerd, always a nerd," and he rolls his antennae at me, giving the same sense as how humans indicate bemusement by rolling eyes.

"All the other wishes can be granted based on Shifter powers, standard stuff, it just takes time," he continues. "Your wish on the other hand, is a whole other story. I will have to tinker a *gnothi seuton* custom solution for you, and that leaves me with not enough time for the rest."

Everyone else glares at me.

"Okay so I'm going to address it this way," says Bonar after a pause. "First, I'll work on activating what Vibe has asked for. He will hold the baton once you reach back home, till further supplies arrive from this end."

"Then, for the three of you, here is how it will play out." He then says looking at Emmy, Joe, and Connie. "In your media history, there is this concept of a military intelligence espionage agent named James Bond. Do you know of him?"

They all nod vigorously, they know this spy guy. Heck, even I have an idea as to who he is.

"For each gig, James Bond gets rigged up with appropriate gadgetry to go fight the bad guys," Bonar continues. "I am going to work out a similar arrangement for you, with the help of our friend Tommy here. You keep thinking up powers you need; and Tommy will make it happen for you. He will make trips back and forth between Visceral Reality and your world."

Tommy grins. He has been having a blast all along this trip. I wish I was his age again.

"Awesome. Now that we can have superpowers, we need code names. Our current names will become our alter egos," Joe says.

He's such a child.

Actually there might be a lesson there. Maybe one should not get hung up on biological age. I have to learn such mental skills from Joe. And hey, it might be fun having code names, why not. It will also serve the purpose of getting us used to our new selves, which will be different from what we ourselves were before, and also different from others around us now. We are no longer our previous selves, and should accept that and come to terms with it properly.

"Well, you are Mojave," I say. "Emmy is Montaña. I'm fine with Vibe, as I've had way too many names thrown at me already. Connie, who are you?"

"Call me The Big Bang," Connie says, "The Ultimate Concepcion."

Look at her, what a name she snagged for herself, huh. She is Bang ... the Big One.

"You are The Conch," Montaña says, looking at me. That's true, that's what I've asked for, and that's what I'm metamorphosing into. I can't hold on to my past either, got to let it go along with the rest. So, for me, Code Name: The Conch.

Oh yes, we're all tripping our way into it.

"We won't need costumes though, per chronology protection we're going to be hundred percent undercover so no other human being will need to know us by a hero identity," Montaña further says jokingly.

"That is correct," says Bonar, while at the same time Mojave interjects with a "hey, why not?"

Bang, Montaña, and I fully process that concept, as we spring back to a degree of solemnness. The imminent extent of loneliness starts to weigh on us. Mojave is the kid, he is still hung up on the costumes consideration. Montaña prods him into attention. Bonar is showing us how the way forward is going to be for our lives, via the Klystron consoles, by means of many different visions. This whole thing is so big, the only way we can catch on and leap along forward is by means of allegorical paths like how Bonar is showing us.

It is also starting to impinge on to our consciousness, that we're soon about to say goodbye to Bonar.

What a fellow.

Why had he visited us? And who is he really? In his own proper time billions of years further out from ours, he is a forest resident, which logically implies he is wild as glory. His trip to our place has also been jungle play, basically.

And we, who have been thinking for a few measly thousand years that we are as civilized as the cat's pajamas, us humans, where do *we* stand again?

That's a sobering thought, and in a way quite a dampener on my sense of well-being. I'm not going to let it get to me though. We're at a party here after all. Let's not have any rain on this parade Bonar has invited us to.

"Vibe, you're good to go now," Bonar announces. "Henceforth, you will be The Conch."

Amazing, I had no idea that I was being worked on. While we've been chatting away about superhero identities and all that, my head just went ahead and got rewired by Bonar in the background, huh.

I don't feel any different. "It won't take effect till you are back home and start to settle in," says Bonar.

"Earlier, you people were asking as to what made me visit you," he continues. "Your world is a significant limit point. I do not know enough about it, but in my time and place, there are people who see visions of the far future, they are known as Mahabodhi Seekers. Some of these visionaries have foretold of a time to come where someone from your solar system journeys forward in time and plays a key role in an apocalyptic event in Visceral Reality. Therefore, although it *is* an extreme journey for someone from my time to undertake and to go that far back into the past, your world nonetheless keeps popping up as a suggested destination for travelers like me who have a hard enough head and thick enough hide to be able to take on the bumpy ride."

Okay, I look around at the rest of the crew, my fellow humans here. We all feel proud, although the detail of the context still escapes us.

"We're the original Mercury astronauts - version 2.0," says Mojave, grinning.

No kidding, that's who we are, in some sense. Back then, it was Houston that worked the machine. In their time, there were those who dissed the astronauts and disparaged their role saying *'even monkeys could do that job.'* But all said and done, the astronauts ruled the roost at the end of the day. Now, in our case, it is Bonar in the driving seat and we all are just enjoying the ride, so it is the same kind of *monkey see monkey do* deal for us as well.

Also, due to the gift of the powers about to be bestowed upon us by Bonar, we could be in the same position as the original Mercury set as far as the rule of the roost for the earth goes. Except that, come to think of it, per chronology protection the citizenry won't know what is going on and hence are not likely to be much impressed by us, so we can pretty much write that one off. That aside, based on what Bonar told us just now, this time we feel proud not just as individuals, but rather on behalf of our species as a whole, and on behalf of this mysterious someone from our solar system who plays a pivotal role in the universe, somehow, at some apocalyptic occurrence.

"Who was this person of whom these visionaries from your time speak of?" I ask Bonar.

"I do not know the name or much of any other detail, but it is said that his home world is Titan, Saturn's moon. Possibly he will be born a millennium or so after your time. That's all I know," Bonar replies. That thought is something for us to take back with us, it feels good.

Hey, now I know why at take-off time Bonar was wondering if our initial revving up would go past Titan! It's something to keep in mind for us too, if we ever have a chance to visit our own near future.

For now, it looks like it is time to go home to our proper time, Planet Earth. Titan is out of reach in our lifespan though, unless via a Visceral shortcut. There is some Lunar and Martian presence, but even that is feasible only for highly specialized scientists and astronauts within our lifetime. That's okay, home sweet home, I'm ready.

Bonar sets up a new machine on the Klystron, as a layer on top of the brachistochrone.

"This is the Vocoder," he tells us. "It will connect with you and talk to you on your return journey, and will guide you along your trip."

Once we reach back, Bang is to tell the folks that Bonar had to go and that he left her with instructions for the continuing Ennyk itinerary.

"I will make the hull of the ship selectively semi-permeable for a short duration," says Bonar, "so that Tommy and I can exit. I will take him to my home, and then once he is ready, send him on for further fantastic adventures. Goodbye now, safe travels. Good luck with saving your world!"

We hug for a good long time. Not sure if it really happened or whether Bonar conjured a sensory experience in our minds for us, but it feels really good.

Then he clicks a button, and the body of the ship shimmers. Our alien friend and the boy in the bubble slowly amble out through the ship's walls while the rest of us stay buckled and strapped. As they are exiting, we can see the bubble shrink, such that eventually it becomes just a body sheath for Tommy. Bonar springs out a device that generates parachutes for both of them, of course more advanced and much simpler and not requiring a bulbous cloth-made dome for the drag. At just the click of a button, they can control the fall.

The ship regains prior form, rigid walls and all. We can remove our restraints now, if we so like.

"Are you ready now for the trip homeward bound?" the Vocoder asks.

We're ready as can be. What other option is there?

So the Ennyk crew will be short a head roadie now, but we will try our best to fill in his shoes.

Back Home

"Okay, you're almost home," the Klystron Vocoder announces briskly. "Hang tight. It's just the last gasp now." The brachistochrone fishbone twitches intermittently during countdown.

My head is in the process of realigning to terrestrial perspectives, much like a bagatelle ball. The others are in a similar boat I'm sure.

We're not ready.

Fight with alien invaders, really? That's what we have to do, when we are back? We're not ready for that.

Oh well, who are we kidding? We've been on this surreal rollercoaster for a while now, and we know that this ride doesn't really end. Ready or not, here we go. We just keep shifting into the next incoming mode, and get face to face with whatever it is.

Like this one, we're here and back to now, our proper time, replete with memories of the future and of far away.

It feels like we're almost still, with just the slightest sensation of motion, like as though we are driving through the Canadian prairies.

"See you later, folks. Maybe," is the last message we hear from the Vocoder, for now at any rate.

Gradually the brachistochrone dissolves and disappears, and the familiar drummers' platforms and the pedestals for the other instruments resume shape, just like how they had been before Bonar had upgraded our ride for an intergalactic scenic detour.

In the shade of a moment, the Klystron turns back into Bang's old faithful truck again.

Back in Bang's old faithful eighteen-wheeler from the days of yore, which was literally yesterday, as we start re-acclimatizing to our old ways and means, it feels like the earth is shaking. I suppose that makes sense since it's the tail end of our return trip and we're still in the process of landing, probably.

But something is wonky with the shakeup we're experiencing. After all, it's not a typical airplane trip; we have traversed the large scale structure of Space-Time, round trip. We do want the earth to be a welcome mat, but it sure doesn't look like one that was laid out on just any ordinary day. Like Galileo said, "And yet it moves." Did we land ourselves back on a magic carpet again instead?

"Hey guys, look around," says Mojave. "The stuff we can see all looks rigid, but why are the shadows moving? When I was younger, as and when the San Andreas Fault acted up, I used to say the earth is quaking. Well, what's shaking and what's quaking now? What do you think?"

Man, after all this we've been through, he's still such a kid. If he got his wish for a costume, come Halloween he'd even go trick or treating, dressed up as his own self! That said, I'm really glad to have him on the team, his swashbuckling attitude will work well for what we have ahead of us.

A few moments elapse, and there's no quake anymore. Around us, it is back now to pretty much the same context as had been when we'd left. It is near dawn; the morning after the night Bonar had taken us all for this glorious trip. I can confirm that based on the date on my watch, which has resumed functioning now, having had been off for the last little while.

"Well, here we are, back at the truck stop," Bang says somberly.

It's what they call Guy Fawkes' Day in some parts of the world. The year is 2102. This day signifies something about someone trying to blow up places, I think.

Supposedly I've got the Conch in my head now. So let me see, what can I explode with that? Nah, I'm not the combustive type. We'll see what my head does, as we go along.

I feel no different from how I was before though, but one thing I do believe with strong conviction. As the Conch now, I am in effect a reincarnated version of Doctor Faustus, having been given one last chance at redemption. If I can help save the world for our kind, then the price of having become one with the Conch, which is in a way the equivalent of the Doctor's attainment of absolute knowledge, would have been paid in full.

But I have to keep such considerations for later. For now it is show time! We're going to get busted by the Orenk any minute per what Bonar said, and the key thing is, we have to stay undercover at least till we get our strategy and tactics in order. We are supposed to docilely say 'uncle' to the anaerobic blob beings, whoever they are, and not flex any muscle.

"You all will be particularly vulnerable since the Orenk will identify you as the prime threat to them soon enough," Bonar had said. "Stay put, and just act like you're worms that are in the beak of a bird but not yet eaten. I'll help you find ways to escape, with Tommy's help. Even if the bird does chop you up into pieces metaphorically speaking, don't worry. I've got your back, as well as the rest of your corporeal substantiation, and I will make sure you regenerate."

Now is the time where this gets put to the test. I'm not sure I'm going to be okay getting chopped up by the bird though, but we'll see.

Ah here we go. The Conch in me is kicking in! I'm starting to receive and process RSS feeds from all around. Not just the media interfaces around us here at the truck stop, but just about any and everything that hits my senses, is automatically getting categorized and classified. The sights and smells and the air quality, the sounds of the birds, the reflections and refractions of the morning sunlight on various surfaces, everything tells me stories now. I'm a living computer, with access points hardwired directly into my head, all kinds of pattern matching and recognition algorithms, and merge sorts and page ranks and all such, going on inside of me.

I'm dizzy and sit down for a bit. My friends seem to know what is going on, and give me space and time to process the change I'm undergoing.

I can hazily see that the Ennyk crew and the rest of the roadies have started to show up. It's a regular morning, from their point of view. Bang runs the spiel by them. The only unusual matter as far as they are concerned, is that Bonar is missing.

"He had to go somewhere," she tells them, "so yes, we're shy a foreman now, but I have got the task lists for the immediate gigs. In the meantime, I'm sure we'll get new orders from the line of command."

"Where's Tomaso?" a woman asks.

"He left with Bonar, Maria," Bang replies. "Not sure what their plan is but it looks like the boy will be away too, for a while."

"Ah, it is probably for the best," Maria shakes her head sadly. "His mother passed away last night."

We all feel the jolt. Bonar probably knew that ahead of time, apparently she was ailing for a while now. Other than her and Memo, the boy had no strong connections here, so might as well show him the cosmos. Well, hope his mother rests in peace.

"Okay, so what's next, Connie?" a plump avuncular gentleman asks. Everyone calls him Uncle Bob.

A little later in the day, the resident band members show up, and Bang introduces us to them.

Julio, the lead vocalist comes over and says "Hello, city slickers. Are you ready to ride with long haired freaky people?" We sure are. He has no idea about the ride we just got off of, though!

Bang brings out the packing slips and bills of lading etc. for a trip south, across the border to Calexico. The Ennyk trip recommences. This time, we will be a part of the experience!

"Well, gang, we're headed for Vegas. That's where the next big gig is," she announces briskly.

We make some road trip time up to Calexico, hosting some bands for tent shows on our way to Vegas, our Winnebago in tow.

It is amusing to see the roadie gang at work. As for Mojave, Montaña, and me we are treated as rookies and hence assigned fairly trivial work. The crew has good camaraderie. One of the girls is saying, "my chancla will be saying hola to your face now," to a persistent young fellow who seems to be pestering her with much fervor. Such is the overall atmosphere.

"What do we have for dinner?" someone shouts. *"Hoya de Pozole,"* is the response from the kitchen area.

We have a good time for a while, all in all.

Then ultimately, as expected, right after we have packed up a show at Brawley, the Orenk's stooges capture us one early morning, just past dawn. It is the 12th of November.

Groggy and dog eared, we are grabbed rudely, and fastened and secured. We all get thrown into the back of a pickup truck. Last but not least, Memo plops down on us all. He is big enough to be able to smother us all in one fell swoop. He is sluggish though; they seem to have tried to render him unconscious but only partially succeeded. We are then taken to what looks to be some cheesy mansion.

In the front hall of the mansion, Carlos the Cholo of whom we've heard accounts from Bang earlier, as also a passing mention by Bonar, is summarily dealing with an obsequious fellow. Carlos has a horde of minions buzzing around like flies.

"Ah, Connie *mi amore,* you are here, and your friends too! Hola, come join the party. Say hello to Juan Lopez," Carlos says smilingly. "He is a nearby Maquila union leader. We had an understanding, but he seems to have forgotten some things, and we are reminding him."

Some of the minions start beating up Juan who begins to whimper and moan as the punishment intensifies. Finally he is let go, and told to leave.

As he crosses the doorway and steps on a metal platform that leads out to the pavement, the metal base rotates a bit, and the poor guy falls down on the base. There is just enough further rotation to make him tumble and hit his head and left shoulder on some protrusions that have sprung out from the moat under the pavement. The protrusions have barbed edges that lacerate the poor guy.

A tall, Slavic looking muscleman brings the metal platform back up, and grabs hold of the poor victim who is cringing and whimpering in pain.

"Vodyanoy, see him off now will you," Carlos says.

As Juan is walking off, Vodyanoy reports in a matter of fact way, "Moderate head bruise and cracked humerus."

"The moat water is mildly poisonous as well," Bang informs us softly, but Carlos has heard what she said. He grins at her amiably, saying "Si, Si Connie... You know it all, my love."

Except for Carlos and his right hand guy Vodyanoy, as for the rest of the gang, all the minions, their lurch is so pronounced that they're practically keeling over all the time. Their recovery of gait is garishly ghastly, a grotesque pantomime. Carlos must have obtained some special dispensation for himself and his right hand man from his Orenk bosses, since their stances are balanced and measured.

Carlos motions to us all to step outside with him and his henchmen. There is breathtaking scenery starting to show up, in the light outside. Not sure if this is how I would have expected the Brawley environs though, something looks alt-dimensional. We are high on a cliff, and a steep descent shows below us, leading down to an as yet dark and silent valley.

Memo is up and about now, and steps across curiously to look over the edge of the cliff, when abruptly Carlos shoots him down.

Memo falls off the cliff side, with a Doppler howl.

We are all numb with shock, can't believe what happened just now.

"This is a warning," Carlos says, with cold menace showing in his eyes. All the earlier affected tone of friendliness is gone. "Connie, I will see you down the line. The rest of you, stay away from our business. We brought you over here, just to tell you that. We know why you were after Connie and I will give you marks for having found her, good detective work and all, but you got into something you don't want to be in, trust me. Not sure as to why she has been giving you the time of day and hanging out with you people though, but whatever it is, no more of it, you understand? Or else you all will go the same way as your dog went. Now scram," He spits on the ground.

We mutely comply, and head out in the Winnebago, Mojave at the wheel.

We can't believe Memo is gone. Everyone is silent, totally at a loss.

The road ahead looks desolate.

"What the hell?" Mojave exclaims in a while.

"Are you okay?" Montaña asks. Mojave's face is contorted in pain.

"My legs!" he screams, grimacing in pain. His foot veers off the pedal, and he crashes the van.

We are all variously injured, the condition is rather critical for each of us I hazily notice. But I'm surprised Mojave felt actual pain, we should all be having Visceral protection. That was basically what Bonar was referring to, as the beak of the bird!

The cartel goons must have done something that made Joe's leg act up, while they were beating us. In fact, they must have done it to us all, since they didn't know who would take the wheel. Yes, I can feel my legs starting to act like a thermocouple; one is turning freezing cold while the other is burning up. This has nothing to do with the crash. Possibly the girls have undergone the same thing, but they have both passed out so I can't confirm. I am fading out too.

The last thing I recollect is the blaring sirens of the emergency response vehicles, presumably called in by someone who came across our crashed vehicle.

When I wake up, there is much hustle and bustle, various hospital staff all running around. The four of us are in an open ward, where there are no other patients.

We all seem to be fine.

"Glad you're up," says Bang.

Per my watch, it shows that the date is the 16th of November. I can't believe I've been knocked out for four days. I am the last one to revive, she says.

Montaña and Mojave are looking out of the windows.

Some support staff members walk in and set us up in wheelchairs. They take us out for a sunshine break. The other patients are all where the hot tubs are, just around the corner. The hospital orderlies seem to have found it expedient to dump us off over this side near the pool, where no one else seems to want to be.

"You don't have to stay in your wheelchairs, your ambulatory functions are normal for all of you. The doctor said you can try stretching your legs. But be careful," a staff member says.

They leave us here and go over to the other side where they can socialize more. The poolside itself is empty except for us.

"Hello again, friends," we hear a low gruff voice, a greeting from the pool.

"Who, what ... who are you?" Mojave says in a startled tone.

"I'm an old dog, come to teach you whelps some new tricks," the voice from the pool says, laughing.

The laughter is modulated with the old baying howl that we have been mourning, the familiar sound of our good friend Memo.

Indeed, it is him, although not physically in person. The impressions I got from the first time we met Memo, around the campfire with Bonar, all come back to me with force. Looking around I see the same flash of recognition in the others, especially Bang since she has known him for longer.

He is back! But how is that possible? And are we dreaming collectively, or is he really here with us?

"You can call me a specter if you like," says Memo, talking to us through the pool water. "By default I do not have a corporeal form. I guess I could adopt a mechanism of mimicry and camouflage, examples of which exist even in the earthly biome of which I once was a part. I could assume the shape of the old dog every now and then, just to make it real for you." As he speaks, the shape of Memo, the big dog we know and love, starts to assume form within the water. He continues talking a human tongue through the pool surface, saying, "Bonar did something similar with his copy of the human form."

We are all agape. The shape of the dog is translucent and ephemeral. Memo conveys a sense of moving his jaws and tongue in sync with what he is communicating, "I'll find ways to modulate my message to you pups as we go along. For this round, this pool will do."

Memo has bounced back from the jaws of death! Not only that, he tells us that he has been our guardian angel seeing us through to safety, from about the time of the van crash.

"What are you all gaping at?" he asks. "You know that Bonar had your back, right? He commissioned your safekeeping to Tommy. But when I was shot at by Carlos, Tommy got my distress call. He came back in a flash and deflected the bullet as best as he could, and then he took me along for a Visceral ride, to fix me up. Then he stayed there for his further journeys, and while sending me back here, he delegated to me his assigned task of taking care of you all."

"Memo, I can't believe it!" Bang says.

"It *is* me, Bang," he replies. "After Tommy had picked me up, he transported me across to a black hole trajectory towards which an Arch-Pivot named Nambu is traveling. From there I have returned back to here, and I now have a touch of the Nambu soul. That allows me to talk to you, and do much more than that as a matter of fact. Do not fret about what I am saying right now, it will all become clear in due time."

Memo's spectral shape waves a ghostly paw across the water. Projected images with metadata tags take shape around the pool, explaining to us in detail as to what he has been saying.

From the projected storyboard he has set up for us, we get to understand that there is a highly evolved universe, even further out in the future than Bonar's time, a time and place where the term Visceral Reality has really come into its own. The name Visceral pertains to the Empire that rules a significant portion of the cosmos at that time. This is the same Empire which is founded by The Nomads, of whom Bonar had been speaking of during our visit to his world. Advanced beings known as Pivots, who are A.I./Animal composites, operate this cosmic scale infrastructure known as Guleil, which is the basis for the strength of this Visceral Empire. Of those Pivots, the most advanced are the Arch-Pivots, of whom this person named Nambu was one, whose soul has now touched Memo.

This is all heavy stuff. Even with the processing capabilities of The Conch, my head is spinning.

"I'm sorry it took me a little longer than I would have liked for it to be," Memo's voice from the pool continues. "Tommy was planning on making it here himself to make sure you guys were all right, but he got intercepted by my episode with Carlos and the bullet, and so he had to take care of matters for me first."

"I can't put it into words how happy I am to see you, Memo," Bang says in a cracking voice.

"Likewise, Connie, you are the dearest among humans for me, right after Tommy that is," says Memo. Dogs always work matters out systematically.

"So, once Tommy intercepted my murder and rescued me off to Visceral Reality," continues Memo, "things changed for me, I have the Visceral touch now."

Thanks to the storyboard he shared with us moments ago, I think I know what he means.

"Memo, it is like you are born again," Bang says.

"Yes, and it is not an ordinary rebirth I have experienced," Memo replies. "As I was telling you just now, Tommy executed a Shifter fly-by for me that further propelled me from where he is (which is the Early-Chilled Era), out to a point in the Mid-Chilled Era where Arch-Pivot Nambu at the end of his life is headed out to a memorial black hole, as a part of his final rites. I then got touched by the soul of Nambu, which imbues me with Visceral Powers the likes of which you cannot even conceive of, even though you have been on a trip with

Bonar to Early Chilled times. My Mid-Chilled Powers are several orders of magnitude greater."

We are still way too dumbfounded to be able to respond much.

"So, as far as taking care of you all is concerned, be assured now. Tommy handed over the baton to me," Memo continues further. "But again, I'm sorry I got a bit delayed reaching you since much was still new to me, and in the meantime, Mojave's legs acted up and your van crashed. I quickly healed as much of your lacerated and mutilated bodies as I could, even before the emergency response units arrived. The hospital people are all amazed at how minor the extent of injury is to all of you, from such a grave crash. I could have fully spirited you off actually, your totaled van included, but it was better to leave you to be discovered by your fellow humans, since the further narrative requires it to be so. But do not worry about anything. I have got your back from now onwards. Before my transformation, humans were my caretakers, specifically Tommy. Now it is my turn, to return the favor to your kind."

So now we are a league of five, Memo being our leader and guardian angel.

We recuperate at the hospital for a bit, just to maintain appearances. Memo could have fixed us up fully as he said, but he guides us to play along with the cartel intent. He then disappears for a while to go get a Visceral recharge for himself, reassured that we should be reasonably safe while at the hospital.

Right on cue though, waiting for us as we are discharged, Carlos's minions are there to scoop us back into their net.

"You people are cats, you have nine lives!" chortles one of the minions. "One life is gone in that van crash, poof! Now let's see what's next for you."

That sounds nice. Where's Memo?

We are again dumped in the back of a rusty pickup truck, taken to some grim industrial looking area, and thrown down on the ground, prodded and poked at till we get up and start walking, and are finally thrust forward and made to walk around the side of a shipyard container, coming face to face with Carlos, again.

Some scrappy hoodlum activities are going on around us in the yard, I notice. There are various harsh cacophonies, clamoring noises, sundry tintinnabulations. My ears hurt.

"Connie, I scalped the woman and got you yours from her, because you got the man for me," Carlos says musingly, bringing my attention back to our situation. "Now, it seems you are required to go back to Beacon and finish the business."

Between the lines, I get my Conch reading. He was the one who got the male beacon outfit. He had murdered the female victim, at about the same time as when Heidi had assassinated the male one. So they both won the rights to the outfits, and she was primary on point in terms of the attempts at breaching Beacon. At some point when she lost her mojo from the cartel point of view, which was about when Bonar had taken her under his wing, this whole Beacon business had been put on the back-burner, and she got temporarily assigned to doing some low end work like driving Ennyk trucks. Now apparently the direction Carlos is getting from his bosses is to resume whatever it is they were planning on doing, with Beacon and its subscriber base, and to continue to use Connie for that purpose.

At least we are allowed to dust ourselves off and relax a bit. It seems like we've been given a reprieve. We hang around the yard, observing the day's activities. Come nightfall, we're left to fend for ourselves in a dilapidated shed.

The minions start to walk off.

"Don't try anything funny," the last of them says to us. "We've got our eyes on you." He leaves, pointing at some closed circuit cameras in the vicinity.

"How did you feel, Bang, when you took someone's life, back when you were a cartel assassin?" I ask later, when there is not much else to do except talk.

"There are so many things that go into the making of people like who I used to be, Conch," she replies somberly. "Think of the influence of the class struggle, for one. A young person in the clutches of poverty can easily be conditioned to come to terms with a point of view that in this war anyone who enjoys the privileges of the rich class is fair game."

"That's a bit drastic," I say gingerly. I should have realized this would be a touchy subject.

"When you see your family and friends being butchered and even massacred en masse around you, the value of life becomes relative," she replies. "In one's value system, taking the life of an 'other' gets rationalized in so many different ways. I never knew who my parents were. My foster parents were killed in a raid when I was a small child, and then I grew up among the cadres of a guerrilla group. By the time I was a teenager, whatever insurgencies were the order of the day which my cadre was involved in, all became meaningless. The people I had grown up with, they either died heartbroken on account of lost causes, or joined the cartel."

I have no idea what to say further.

"Still, I don't mean to imply that what I did for the cartel is understandable or excusable, Conch, I know it was wrong," she continues. "With the help of Bonar, I now know better and have acquired higher level values. I have done time in my head, and have moved forward," she pauses for a moment before continuing:

"There is an Ennyk song I sing to myself sometimes,

I have my guilt I got my regrets
I skated around them, and did some Figure Eights…
Such as it is,
Now I'm at peace." She looks hazy eyed and far away.

I can't think of anything to say. We just watch the moon go down for a bit, and then curl up into a somewhat convoluted spoon and hug each other for a long time. But neither of us is at peace, really. Montaña and Mojave are similarly huddled up a few feet away from us.

The next day rolls along as usual, like as though nothing is out of the way or out of place at all.

Well, except that we have woken up in a dirty little shed, and are again captured and tied up and get kicked at and beaten up. It's getting to be annoying.

Carlos then sets up what seems to be a rather elaborate torture session for us. His minions are grinning wickedly, even drooling! We have a special kind of noose around each of our necks and are hung up while standing on rickety stools and end tables.

Had we not been touched by Visceral Reality, I doubt if any one of us would have been able to withstand what all is going on. As things stand, we are all play acting the roles of victims of terror. I am able to watch all this in an 'out of body' way and be the actor as required in this role play game, and I sense that the rest of the group are doing the same, pretty much. Between Bonar, Tommy, and Memo, our guardian angels have rigged up our defenses well.

"If it were up to me I would probably finish off at least some of you, if not all," Carlos says, smiling thinly. "But I have my orders, and you all are to be held by the sword." That sounds icky, but we were expecting something like this anyway.

The nooses tighten around our necks.

My Conch instinct kicks in and I start to act like I'm acquiring the loping gait and the associated mannerisms. The others catch on and do the same. Bang especially has background knowledge from her cartel days, and she does a bang on job, pun intended, in terms of putting on the act.

My conch engine is running on overdrive. Amongst the infected and inflicted human beings, we have come across who have displayed these symptoms to date, including, and up to the rag tag bunch we've seen out and about in this yard, I see a spectrum of the extent to which the manubrium bond has taken over a person. There are lopers, and then there are e-lopers; the latter being extreme lopers who have crossed the point of no return. This is what Carlos means, by us being held by the sword. We are about to be anointed in some fashion, and force-converted into fellow scum.

Upon becoming held beyond the point of extreme lope, humans start looking alien, still breathing and burping but differently, trading in their carbon heritage for new ways of metabolizing, incrementally, little by little.

Now with this noose thing, we too are being fast tracked into e-loper status, and need to start showing this alien anaerobic behavior now.

The minions bring out equipment with which they pump in chemicals into us, and clumsily take readings of our conditions.

I was right; this was exactly what they were looking for, the onset of this behavior for the four of us!

This technically is my very first comprehensive internal conch measure that includes an outtake. Without an igloo or a mobile, I got the whole analysis together in my head! It's thrilling.

But no room to thump my chest, it is crunch time now.

Indeed, the way the infection is spreading all across the world makes it evident that there is an extremely sinister intent behind this epidemic, which is well beyond the current reach of human ability.

Carlos and the rest of these guys have undoubtedly become stooges of the Orenk, who have the ultimate means of controlling the extent of infliction. But these people would have to be fairly up in the hierarchy in terms of the source of this scourge, close enough to the real villains I would assume, since they have been trusted with this key knowledge of directly infecting targeted humans like us.

Carlos has us by the throats, as we're still on the nooses. The throat grab seems to be a literal need for the deployment of the infection. He measures our mimicked change, checking for the loping gait, the crooked smile, and the haze in the eyes.

Some more nasty chemicals are shoved into our metabolisms. Bonar's and Memo's filters save us from any real damage, but the process itself and the peripheral effects are quite bothersome.

Finally, it looks like we're done.

First Montaña, then me, then Mojave and lastly Bang. He lets us off the noose one by one, and we feign allegiance as per his directions.

"I would have taken some toll," he says. He means he would have maimed us or even killed us. What the hell, he even did attempt to do so, by making our van crash. "But my instructions are to convert you," he continues, "because you seem to have some sleuthing skills which might be useful for some janitorial tasks we have, at least out at this Beacon shop, and my chain of command seems to be willing to give you a chance. So, you all are slotted to head over to L.A. now, and await further instructions."

The Ennyk crew would have made it to Las Vegas by now. I wish we were continuing as roadies with them, rather than in this gooey mess.

Carlos and his cronies kick us around, slap our butts, and scratch our faces, accompanied by jeers and guffaws. It is annoying, but Memo has strictly advised us to just play along for now.

In order to defeat the Orenk, humankind needs to get its act together. That is the task for us now, to guide our kind along this path and lead the war. On the one hand, we have to fake being under this manubrium bond thing, whatever it is, and continue our janitorial duties. On the other hand, we do our hero stuff, undercover. If someone gets a hint of our powers, chronology protection will distance them from us and we keep getting lonelier and lonelier as we go. Awesome isn't it, huh.

Well, at least the trip to Bonar's world gave us the vim, and vigor and vitality that should help tide us over this grim picture. Also it has enhanced our perspective and acumen. Plus, we will have these powers to play with, once Memo gets around to the disbursal. We'll make the best of it, stiff upper lip, chin up, and all that. We're not going to let the earth get decarbonized.

Game on.

Role Play

"Now, let's see how sharp you are on the streets," Carlos says, with a smile that is as thin as his moustache. "Go forth and proliferate the mayhem, children. You head on over to Joe's house in L.A. In a while we will catch up with you there, and will then pull back on your hold enough for you to be sufficiently presentable socially speaking, to go to Beacon and do our bidding."

Being The Conch, I can read between the lines, and interpret the gist of what is to come.

So, it's role play time. We're expected to show evil behavior. They want to see how effective we are, as their sulfur infused lab rats. And then they will suppress our lope such that we can find ways to infect the Beacon subscribers on their behalf, and hack through the blocks Bonar had put in at Beacon for their subversion attempts, basically.

It would be challenging now to continue to orchestrate the mimicry even for this first leg of mayhem proliferation that we're being sent out to do, since the physical manifestations on the infected body are complex with the onset of extreme lope. There are various nauseating protuberances, warts, boils. Memo will have to pull some strings at a cosmic level to achieve the necessary. Ordinary makeup and masks won't do.

Vodyanoy sees us off, slapping us silly all the way out the door.

We're set to go, on our way out. Will we make it past the moat?

Yes we do, the metal platform at the moat crossing stays stable. Amazing, Carlos has let us go!

"Bloody idiots," Montaña snaps. "They've built a tacky little Gormenghast here, for what? Are they afraid the neighboring cactus population will come creeping upon them on some witchy night, and storm the keep?"

Wow man, I've never seen her so angry.

We lurch our way along, just like real legitimate e-lopers in the initial stages of our transformation.

"Well we slipped past that one I think," Bang says, once we've turned a corner and are approaching our Winnebago.

"Don't assume too much," I caution.

"Okay, since you are representing Tommy," she says to Memo, who quietly takes shape just ahead of us, joining us as we walk towards the van, "and will help us out on his behalf with the task Bonar had assigned to him, namely to boost us up with superpowers, here is my first James Bond gadget requisition. You know the spy guy Bonar was talking about?"

Memo growls an affirmative. As a Viscerally touched being of terrestrial origin, he now has way deeper knowledge of human culture and all that stuff, than we can even imagine.

"This spy analogy is rather fitting, especially since we've been assigned an industrial and corporate espionage mission now by Carlos," she continues further. "So anyway, I'm sure we will have to change our appearances a heck of a lot more in this war, for various reasons, and quite rapidly at that. I'll use the term subterfuge shots for what I have in mind. That aside, even for this immediate situation, soon we will need to show extreme lope and we can't fake that without your help. In short, Memo, can you get us the power to morph our outer bodies as per need."

Talk about being in lockstep. She had the exact same thought that I was mulling on just now!

"Hold on with your shape shifting requirement there for a moment, young lady," Memo pulls in the reins a bit. "I'm not going to do packet switching for each such requisition that you people come up with, and keep going between *here and now* and the other side. This is not IP telephony, you know. I am connecting you to the far future. Make a list, all of you, and I'll execute in one trip, in one shot. Like Bonar had said, you only go to the well once. I already have the items you were requesting Bonar for, which he had said Tommy will take care of for you. Now I got the baton from Tommy so I got those already."

"Hey, how do you know what Bonar had said to us?" Mojave asks.

"My friend, did you think Bonar spun up a communication mechanism only for you humans? He was well versed in dog speak. I knew what was going on, throughout the trip," Memo laughs. That makes sense.

Interesting, Memo classifies what Bang has asked for, as a request for the ability to shape-shift. Come to think of it, so it is. Related to that, something further comes to my mind though.

"There is one fine tuning to this requirement that I want to submit," I say.

Memo looks at me in such a way that I can see that he already knows where I'm going with this. I continue anyway, for the benefit of the rest.

"In addition to the need for changing our appearances and grow the necessary warts and boils to allow us to perform the cartel duties while pretending to be held by the sword, whatever *that* means," I continue, "like Bang said, going forward we will be changing our guises quite a bit, in other ways too, with the intent being disguise and camouflage for purposes of war, for the missions that will come our way. Therefore, can you set each of us up with personal signatures such that we can recognize each other no matter what human forms our outer guises show for each of us?"

Memo laughs heartily. A wave of mirth engulfs all of us, courtesy of his Arch-Pivot powers.

"You children will not get lost. Don't worry, you've got me!" he says while laughing. "But that's okay. It might be fun, let me set you all up."

"Montaña will heat up the surroundings mildly," he gets on the job right away, his wizardry is in action even as we walk. We can see it happening around us as he is speaking.

"Mojave will bring just a touch of an arctic level freeze blast to those around," Memo continues. On cue, the cold blast kicks in at us.

"Bang will have an attractive pressure gradient with people attracted to her but she will be able to hold them at bay," then says Memo, "and she will be accompanied by a certain whistle in the wind which I can also hear wherever I am, a bit of a personal touch since she is the human I am next imprinted to in the absence of Tommy."

Everyone is manifestly drawn towards her, like maybe she's an elf.

"As for you, Conch, last but not the least," I can feel it that Memo has it in for me and is setting me up, "you will be the center of a pressure gradient that repels, thus providing you with the necessary elbow room in your mind for what you have to do."

That doesn't sound cool.

"You will all be equipped with Pressure/Temperature sensors that will help you recognize each other, irrespective of the outer corporeal bearing," Memo finishes off.

"Are you saying you're going to make me repulsive?" I say, with indignation that is only in part mock. Even as we speak, the rest of the crew except for Bang has adjusted themselves and their positions in such a way as to give me more room. It hits me with an extra touch of loneliness. Don't tell me even *these* guys are going to keep their distance from me. Bonar has already explained the implications of chronology protection and how isolated we as a group are set to become. Now even within the group I'm set apart alone.

"It's all right, I'll take care of you baby," Bang pulls me towards her. Her attractive gradient nullifies my repulsion. At least I have that.

Memo scares us all with a howling roar. We slowly realize that he is laughing. "Dude, trust me, solitude is good. You are the Conch, you will need the room in your head, considering what all goes on in there," he says.

I mull on that.

"I will remove the constraints of the pressure / temperature sensors amongst yourselves, when you already recognize each other," says Memo. "They will kick in only when you feel the inability to identify one another." Indeed, he is like a godparent for us now.

"You know what, Bang, I can already foresee some ugly situations where you will need this shape morphing skill for more urgent matters as well," Memo further weighs in, musingly. "As a SWAT team championing your world, you people will soon have to take some drastic actions, such as defusing nuclear warheads. To do that, you will need to morph into the shape of other humans, including faking their biometric signatures for sensors to get access to where you can thus defuse."

Ah, funny that he should mention that. I too can sense imminent fissile disturbances. Not a happy situation, but might as well come to terms with it and figure out how to solve the problem.

"Here's my requisition. I want to be able to move stuff around," says Montaña. "So for example, if someone innocent is in the line of fire, I want to be able to deflect the bullet and save their life."

Memo nods. Check, he's got it.

"What about the base model features," Mojave asks meanwhile. "Like the ability to fly out into space and walk through things and see through things and scale buildings and have extraordinary strength and all that? Do we need to individually requisition all of that?" He knows the drill with all this superhero stuff.

"Yes fine, we'll see how to rig you all up for all that, all in good time," Memo grumblingly obliges. "Let's start with the flying; I'll give you a little spring in your walk, along with some GPS fluid modulated onto your blood vessels. The GPS in you will receive Viscerally programmed position information from the nearby celestial objects, no need for an artificial satellite. With that in place you can hop your way around here on Earth, via the troposphere."

"Can you please make it a simple aerodynamic solution, no clunky jetpack stuff?" Mojave pipes in further.

"Okay, an order of gossamer angel wings for you, coming right up," says Memo, dripping sarcasm.

"But always remember the impact chronology protection will have on your contexts and situations every time you invoke any such power," he continues. "It will mess up your day to day interactions with fellow mortals, since they can never become aware of any Visceral influence on your world or time. That is forbidden."

"So, for example," Memo elaborates, "if there is a risk of some other human seeing you flying around with no jetpack, events will conspire in such a way as to prevent that occurrence. The extent to which someone else does get exposed to the effects of your power, for example if they see the dust you raise as you take off, to that extent, further events will take shape so as to keep them away from you. In short, the likelihood diminishes, of your paths crossing going forward. In effect, this means that with the people whose trajectories you happen to intercept while exercising your powers, the chances of future interactions will gradually reduce. This means that step by step you will be forced into solitude and just have each other from within this group for company, and the odds of becoming close with any other human will recede with each such likely occurrence."

That is a really grim prospect indeed.

In effect, we will be living a parallel reality, incrementally getting distanced from the one we were born in, wherein we will eventually become ghosts.

That aside, not sure how much fun it will be, flying out to the troposphere and having x-ray vision and all that, when the rest of humankind is dying below us. But we need the tools of the trade, fun or not.

"I can taste the ashes in my mouth," I say. They all know what I mean, even Mojave.

The show must go on. We, our world and all of us, are under siege.

In a moment of Conch inspiration, it becomes clear to me as to what being *held by the sword* actually means. They're referring to the Xiphoid, the cartilaginous extension in the human sternum. The Orenk hold us by the Xiphoid process in our bodies, the sword in our sternum. *That* is how they are controlling us. Once they grab us there, they control us and can play us however they want. We become like puppets on a string. That is what all the lopers on the street are, basically.

They get hold of the Xiphoid in us, by means of infecting us through the manubrium. The rest is just like spinal tap, but triggered from up at the neck end. It is wicked indeed.

This was what Bonar had meant when he referred to the Manubrium Bond, during our first debrief at the campfire way back when. The Orenk get at us through the scruff of the neck. And from in there, they then grab us by the sword in our sternum and make puppets out of us. They turn us into de facto zombies under their control. This is seriously wicked stuff.

"We're going to need some heavy duty powers to be able to fight this, Memo," I raise the flag. "We will need to be able to reclaim the human race from the brink of extinction, and prevent the rest of the earth biome too from being subject to drastic modification. It is not a small matter, we will ultimately need the power to control life force at large at least at the scale of the entire earth, and defend our biome, and not die out."

"I'm already on it," Memo replies tersely. He usually knows what is coming, well ahead of time; he has the touch of an Arch-Pivot after all. We can see as well that he is busy on the job. It seems to be a painful laundry list he's taking on for us. But he's our buddy, he's got our back. We can sense him appear and disappear back and forth along whatever spectral pathways that he goes on, presumably for the task of setting us up with our powers.

But we're not heading out for a joy ride, not in any sense. Our survival is at stake on the earth. Not just for the human species, but for all carbon based life here.

Well, got to get on with what the day has in store for us in the meanwhile. We stop at a coffee shop in Brawley. Memo has stepped over to Visceral Reality and will be back shortly.

The TV is on. A perky little girl with a quirky smile is holding a microphone, answering a reporter's questions. She seems amused for some reason, her left eyebrow shoots up, and in conjunction, her left hip juts out starboard. They seem to be covering preparations for a parade.

"The coming weekend is Thanksgiving," Mojave says, deducing from what is being discussed on TV.

"You know, as a species, I think it is time that we humans should look at adjusting this weekend," Bang responds to his comment. "Maybe re-designate either Black Friday or Cyber Monday as the Day of Remorse. In any case, we all should cut down a bit on the consumerism aspect of it. One day should suffice for shopping and deals, come on."

"What do you mean by remorse though?" I ask.

"Well, giving thanks for all that is plenty and bountiful in the land is a good thing for sure," Bang replies looking at Montaña, who seems to already know what she means, "whether for the hosts who live off the land already or for guests who have come to stay. But it is a bit incongruous to be thankful for what was received from the native people, when their populations nearly got wiped out in the exchange. That whole situation calls for some serious remorse. So let's designate a day for the purpose."

There is a moment of uncomfortable silence. This concept cuts through a major swath of human culture and history, after all.

"Let me take a shot at being the Advocate Diaboli," Mojave says in a while. "By and large, the native populations in America were fierce people, they were warriors. In the wars that took place, it so happened they drew the short straw. In any war, some die and some live on. Isn't that in the natural order of things, historically speaking?"

"Not every native who died of a European gunshot was a warrior," Bang responds forcefully. "Several peaceful tribes were enslaved for purposes of profit, under the terror of example deaths by gunfire. It was not an honorable war everywhere. Much of it was just evil greed, rather similar to what these Orenk are doing now to our world. You can't seriously question the need for remorse in this context, man. Come on!"

I find myself out of depth and at a loss for words, just keep sipping my coffee, letting the others speak.

"Even assuming that it is an acceptable thing to have used firearms to kill off those who were wielding bows and arrows and tomahawks," Montaña continues the argument, "that is not the only point in the case Bang is making. We also have to look at what happened thereafter. Look at the way the surviving native people were done in with firewater and rum, and how that has continued on one way or the other, even up to modern days, what with crystal meth and all. That whole thing has been a sociological and anthropological play of guile and deceit. That might even have had a bigger hand in the decimation of the native populations, even more so than the early battles."

As we are talking, we finish up at the coffee shop and get back into the van. Not going anywhere yet, but the Winnebago is our base for now. Soon we do have to head out for L.A. though, per Carlos' diktat.

"Well, the invention of firearms is a testament to the ingenuity of the white people," The devil's advocate continues. "Every race of humans has had some form of weaponry in their toolset along the course of history, and you can't really blame someone for having invented a better set of tools. Weapons get used in wars, one side wins and the other side loses. It is the way history plays itself out. I'm not taking any moral stance here. Wrongs do occur in human interactions, and history sometimes provides corrective arcs, sometimes it doesn't. All I'm saying is that remorse on behalf of some long gone ancestors might just end up being misplaced energy. We might be better off investing that focus towards attaining the best possible policy solutions for today's world."

"The world today does need help," I can't help but agree with that. We are all children of anarchy, this generation of ours, and could use all the help we can get.

"As for your other point," Mojave continues, "can we really blame the addictions of those who received the abusive substances, on those who provided the said substances? Yes, whiskey is a European invention, but the nature of use and the effect of it will depend upon the user, isn't it?"

"I'll answer your second question first," Bang responds. "It is a fairly universally accepted principle of law that the crimes of the dealers and pushers are far graver in nature than those of the consumers of the drugs. Trust me on this, I'm a cartel girl. The core problem is the nefarious intent of running an entire group of people into the ground, and that too not only by means of an overt war, but also under the radar, done in a regular day's work just by getting them hooked on to some form of poison or the other. No doubt that along the way native tribal chiefs have partaken of the guilt as well by selling their own people out, but the root intent has been that of the prevailing establishment. The tribal chiefs who succumbed to bribes are but pawns in the game."

She pauses for a minute before continuing. "Secondly, there is no denying that in the course of recent history the white race has been ingenious and enterprising and all that. The origins of that can well be traced back to the industrial revolution. But even for that, on the flip side of that exact same spirit of enterprise are the ecological problems which we are seeing today, that are attributable to the concomitant fast-track use of earth's resources. Nature got short-changed along the path of modern civilization, on account of human greed. No denying that ingenuity has its place in the scheme of things, but it shouldn't come at the price of inner balance. Someday we will pay the price for it, unless we apply corrective measures."

"I don't disagree with you there," says Mojave. "But I still believe that we should focus on looking forward and facing the future, and fix up our governmental policies based on lessons learned from the past, rather than getting hung up on the historical misdeeds of generations long gone."

"I'm not saying that within the context of our human ethnicities we have to perpetuate the enmities," Bang says thoughtfully. "In a family, when brothers fight, the one who hurts the other says sorry at some point, and compensates in some fashion to make his sibling feel better. That is how families grow stronger together. So, extending the logic to larger cross-ethnic contexts, from this example of within a single family out to all of humanity, I believe a designated day of remorse will help with that goal, such that for our future generations, the human race will be a healthier family overall."

No one can say much in response to that. These are real heavy matters.

Memo rejoins us in the meantime. "Got the juice for you," he says.

"Ah, time to test our powers," Mojave exults.

"All in good time my friend, I will let you know when to flex which muscle," Memo tempers the flame.

We all try to settle back into the van, old familiar positions for most of us. Bang is the new member of the Winnebago family. As to Memo, he is a specter; he is in and out at will, doesn't occupy room.

My situation is funny. I'm now the Conch personified, but still I was not able to comprehend Bang's thought about Thanksgiving and racial conflicts, till she elaborated upon it. I can pin point solutions for objective situations in a flash now, but in terms of direct communication with people, I'm still the same old introverted Vibe, can't connect easily. I must admit I feel really inspired by my friends. Even in this situation of global chaos and alien invasion, they are able to think through significant philosophical matters and draw out considerations of future policies for the world.

In particular, Bang makes a strong point. Something is seriously screwed up in the wiring inside our heads, us human beings as a whole. As a species, we do need to continuously apply corrective measures to our evolutionary trajectory, and a mix of gratitude and remorse is probably a good state to aim for in general. Can we ever fix ourselves and become better beings? Are we really trending up, evolutionarily speaking? Who knows.

Right now though, we don't have time on hand to think of such finer matters. The immediate priority is to deal with the grim problem of the possible extinction of humankind and the associated biome that is staring at us in the face.

"Hey Conch, do you still need your old conch apparatus?" asks Mojave. "If not, we can make room in the Winnebago. It is a long way back to L.A., we could use the space."

"Go for it," I tell him. The whole reason I had asked for this gift of internalizing the Conch from Bonar was to stop being limited and constrained by all that clutter.

"Hey Memo, how about Montaña tests out the power she has asked for?" he enquires. "She can do her magic, can't she? Move stuff around locally?"

"Yes, once Memo confirms I got the mojo, I guess I could deploy the stuff to the miscellany stock of various nearby hobbyists and electronics and other instrumentation enthusiasts' garages once the Conch identifies them for me with his wizard mind," she says. "I'm sure it'll make a lot of them happy."

"Don't do that yet," Memo steps in. "As we move along and fight battles, our friend The Conch might be otherwise occupied on occasion, and we might need Montaña to operate the old Conch apparatus to capture the identities of people we rescue along the way, so that we can make use of that to save them from the lopers."

Mojave doesn't quite follow, but he goes along with it. The stuff stays.

Based on what Memo said, I see and anticipate a role which I will have to play myself too, for which Montaña will be my backup and she will be using the machinery when I'm otherwise busy. The thought makes my heart heavy. People's lives will be at stake. It should work out all right though; after all, we ourselves have gone through that forge and fire. But this time it will be us at the helm instead of Bonar. We will be guided by Memo of course.

There is history behind how the Conch captured people's identities. Of course, Bonar's purpose in designing it that way was precisely to allow us to partake of the Shifter ride on the Klystron at the right time.

People and their identities have traveled along strange currents along history.

A few generations ago, the establishment wanted to aggressively spy on the people, Big Brother and all that. The people were provided with some soporific or the other, and they gradually got more and more numb, and forfeited their privacy bit by bit.

And then there was a backlash period where political revolutions happened around the world, attempts at a new world order. The people then suddenly woke up with a sense of loss for the identities they felt they'd surrendered, and shut themselves in, trying to rediscover their private selves – you could call it the age of islands.

Then came our generation, and the pendulum swung back again. People somehow voluntarily started to put it all out there, everybody's hearts were worn right out on their technological sleeves. It was in this context that we invented the Conch. People willingly shared their identity with the Conch, and Bonar modulated on top of that in such a way that the Shifter could give you a ride once you funneled your Conch identity into it. With their identity thus externalized, life-forms can undertake a Shifter trip, riding on Quantum Field Theory over Curved Space-Time. Once you share yourself with the Shifter, it can map you.

The Shifter maps to alternate projections of the Super-Symmetry-heavy counterparts for each particle from a given person's set of quantum fields. That is how you hitch a ride. We ourselves saw it in action with the Klystron ride we took.

There is a hefty load of science, technology, engineering, and mathematics to it of course.

For the identity of a person: inter alia, there are the following Self-adjoint operators we used in design of the Conch:

- Peace
- Happiness
- Power
- Contentment
- Lust
- Appetite
- Passion
- Adventure
- Excitement
- Reason
- Thrill
- Ecstasy

As you start to understand what each of the above mean to a person, you essentially get a map of their core being. Padding on the flesh and blood on top to recreate a person is a piece of cake for a Visceral being like Bonar, or now Memo.

It is not just the parsing of the above extensible set of self-adjoint operators though, mapping a person is a fairly involved exercise. That was why Bonar had orchestrated the entire conch gig that brought us back into contact with him, and in the process, the personalities of our duals in the Conch matured enough for him to be able to properly map us for the trip he took us along on.

I see what Memo means in terms of potentially utilizing this apparatus to save the lives of any victims we come across in this war, but it worries me as to how we will be able to map such involuntary hitchhikers at short notice.

Well, Memo has the touch of an Arch-Pivot soul after all, and I now have a rough idea what that means. I will trust him on this.

As a beneficial side effect, this will grow our cadre as the Visceral empowered league defending the Earth, and we as a team will be less lonely as we go. It is tragic though that the new folks are being brought in not at their will, but the alternative for them would have been death anyhow, so we can't really feel too upset about it. In some sense at least, we would have saved them.

Anyway, coming back to the now and here, as I shake off my whimsical daydreaming state of mind, I see that the others have prepared us for the journey, and we are about to set off.

We step out on the road. It is time to check out everything with our newborn eyes, got to get on with the business on hand and win back the world for ourselves.

We reach L.A. just before the weekend, through the worst possible series of traffic nightmares. Bang is driving, using her eighteen wheeler expertise. We are heading for Mojave's house, all of us exhausted from the bumper to bumper hell ride. We turn from 35th Ave onto Hermosa Avenue, and then take the raised ramp out to the ferry dock. The ferry operator whistles softly looking at our van, probably wondering how to fit it in, but he manages.

This is the time when many of the neighbors are reaching home at Mojave's housing complex. Everyone gets off the ferry and walks off into respective houses, and their cars work out exit protocols and park themselves. There are various degrees of autonomy for the vehicles. But our rented Winnebago does not have the necessary features for IoT (Internet of Things) integration with the ferry control panel, so we have to wait for when the traffic is sparse, to let ourselves in manually.

"Who all lives here?" Montaña asks.

"The neighbors in the complex are a mixed bag," says Mojave. "Some are Chariot colleagues, some Hollywood fringe people, and some other miscellaneous junta. I don't know everyone of course."

We settle into his apartment, but no one is at ease considering the hell that is about to break loose soon enough. Bang and I take one room while Mojave and Montaña settle into his master bedroom.

I submit to the exhaustion and fall asleep right away.

In the morning, I see that it has been pretty much the same story with the rest as well.

"Hey Conch, terrorism usually targets large public events. Do you see a risk arising at the Thanksgiving Parade in New York?" Mojave asks.

I crunch the likelihood and say, "Not specifically." The Orenk attack on our world is different from the typical forms of terror we have known hitherto.

As we're talking, the apartment door opens.

It's Randy Logan. "Hello, children," he smiles, oily face and all.

"Heck, how did you get in?" Mojave expostulates. "Never mind, what am I saying? You have your means."

Randy sets about decimating the breakfast platter, which was supposed to be the meal for all of us.

"Hey buddy, now that we are a part of the family, would you mind enlightening us as to who are our ultimate bosses?" I ask.

"Now look here, malai kofta," says Randy in response. "You are neither a compass nor an atlas, why do you care where your orders come from? Besides, the family house is way out of reach for you. Even the dog house is several steps of ascension away from where you are at."

The condescension drips from his tone like a dog's drool.

The benefit of being the Conch is that I can right away decode all the subliminal messages that come across with what someone says. Randy is originally from South India. My origins on the other hand, are from an Eastern state in India. The term he used to refer to me, *malai kofta*, is a cuisine item from North India, where malai refers to cream. But in *his* Southern language, malai means mountain, or maybe a hill. My roots are from a hilly region of the country, and hence his use of that term for me is in effect to call me a hillbilly. In India, there is further salt to that wound though, since tribal people from the hills like my kind, have historically been suppressed and exploited by the folks of the plains, unlike in America where they ride the big waves and have even made it to Beverly Hills and raked in the Hollywood millions.

It isn't all that pleasant really, being The Conch. I now sense and know what is between the lines, which more often than not, I'd rather not. Well, I asked for it, so it's my cross to bear. Mental note to self: stop whining.

Anyway, coming back to Randy, he is not going to tell us anything about the chain of command. He hates me for sure. I still haven't gauged his feelings for the others. He is here following his own orders I suppose, and will torture and torment us while he is at it, just for kicks.

Why do we have to deal with him at all? He irritates me to no end.

Damn it, Carlos sent us on a long tiring drive from Brawley back to L.A., just so that Randy could have some fun with us. It is really infuriating, but we have to lie low.

While walking around the apartment and talking to us, Randy whips out his blade here and there and causes various lacerations on our bodies haphazardly, "for old time's sake," as he calls it, even though supposedly we're on the same team now. It is his way of showing who is boss. Also, I get the Conch reading that his blade is imparting a temporary antidote to the sword hold, such that we can be socially presentable at The Beacon.

"Carlos and I, we both thought that you people are not worth our while," Randy says disdainfully while walking out the door, signaling for us to walk along with him. "The way you have mucked around with our business, either of us would have finished you off in a moment, with no second thoughts. But someone up the chain seems to believe that your background with Beacon Inc. can be of use."

He pauses, and smiles thinly at our feigned looks of relief. Damn, we are getting good at role play. We know now the Memo will bail us out at the slightest hint of harm coming our way so we're not really scared, but are doing our best at play acting per his expectations.

"We find that resistance is developing amongst the targets, in the contexts of the other technologies that we have infiltrated," Randy says while crudely harassing Montaña and Bang, as we are all getting ready to step out. "So, when we do penetrate Beacon, their signature jacket might not be enough anymore. We have to get the Beacon subscribers to mandatorily get into BDSM, and make choke collars a part of the offering."

"That won't fly," says Mojave. "Customers won't see the connection, so marketing won't sell it. By the time someone puts on *that* kind of gear, they're well past the stage of interaction where the Beacon technology has a bearing. Beacon scope is basically prior to and up to the point of arousal. By the time someone is putting on BDSM gear, they're already getting it on, and hence are past the Beacon strike zone, from a marketing point of view. So we might as well just directly hit the fetish shops instead of Beacon, if that is where the focus is to be."

Randy looks at him for a moment, and nods.

"I see your point. The fetish shops are already in our basket as a matter of fact, but that is a relatively small subscriber base," he says. "So, it *is* time we take over Beacon and somehow make it work for us," he continues. "It is just that I personally don't think *you* people have it in you to pull it off," he sneers at us. "But, you're being given a chance by the chain of command, so I will hold my judgment for now. You do have some advantage, since

Emmy works there, and malai boy has done some business deals as well with Beacon, so let's see how you all do."

We all step out of the apartment. Mojave locks up his house and walks forward to join the rest of us while glaring furiously at the back of Randy's head.

In the corridor there is a young woman, a petite brunette.

"Kill her," Randy says quite arbitrarily and abruptly, throwing me a gun, another one pointed right at my head. He is testing me.

I knew something like this was coming. But that doesn't make it any easier.

Where are the gods? This is the very crossroads. I have to take a life now, or forfeit mine? What happens if I don't? *Memo, I hope you got it*, I beseech in my mind.

"Stall as much as you can," Memo's voice whispers in my head.

"Joe, what is this?" the woman screams in fear.

In a flash, I recognize her. She was one of his fellow actors in that Chariot gig I'd undertaken way back when. Oh, Glory! She has a valid Conch dual then. Using that, Memo can whisk her over to Visceral Reality, as long as we time it right. I won't be committing murder.

"Joe, you know her?" I ask him.

"She's my neighbor, man, and a Chariot colleague," Mojave replies. He is visibly agitated.

"Okay, I got her mapped," Memo's voice taps me from within. That is even better! He's touched by the soul of an Arch-Pivot after all; he's got it covered on his own. The Conch dual can just be for backup, in case he needs fine tuning touches later. I hesitate for just a moment, and squeeze the trigger. She screams once more, and moans. Silence follows.

Randy cackles with delight, and slaps me on my back in mock camaraderie. The woman's accusatory gaze as she was fading off, tortures me. I fervently hope that I will have occasion to explain myself to her soon, once Memo revives her.

"You all go on, I'll clean up here," Memo's voice booms in my head.

Slowly I drag myself towards the exit door behind Randy who also luckily has decided to move on, and everyone follows.

Society is in shambles, it is crumbling in front of us. We can see the effect right here. Mojave's apartment complex is high end, best in class kind of thing. Even here, we see no response from any form of authorities. Surely security camera feeds must have captured what apparently was a murder? Of course, it has only been a couple of minutes or so, but for me it feels like we've been dangling on an eternity all through this occurrence. How come no alarm?

Anyway, we walk on.

The others avoid me, until suddenly they each start to seek me out for eye contact. I figure Memo has explained the matter to them individually. Well, that is a relief.

Randy then hands us a knife each, and makes us cut up some random people in the streets, maybe to mark our targets for future reference. My Conch reading is that these knives are spiked with Orenk venom. It clicks in my head that these people will also be in for a Klystron ride at some point. "You're right, I've got them covered too," Memo's whispering voice continues in my head. "We'll have Montaña spin up their Conch duals when she can, just for backup."

We are then instructed by Randy to head over to New York, to go and complete the infiltration into the Beacon network. It is a funny coincidence that Mojave was raising a concern just a little while back about the parade there. Here we are, going to New York anyhow.

This time we are to fly, so we head out to the airport in a cab.

We look a wicked bunch indeed, prime e-lopers every one of us. But we all hate having to go through this pretension.

Who likes to be on the wrong side, anyway?

As it is, people of the earth are fast becoming strangers to each other. The lopers are predatory in nature, and we now are to show ourselves as a part of their ranks and prey upon fellow humans. There is eternal enmity between good and evil, and we now are positioned on the dark end of the spectrum. The very thought comes with a foul taste in the mouth.

Of our kith and kin, those who as yet don't have the manubrium bond hold will abhor and fear us just as they do the other lopers. Those already held by the sword on the other hand, will consider us as fellow thugs who have joined them in the zombie ranks. That's just great, huh.

For Montaña and me, this is less of a concern. Our immediate folks in the sense of family and friends are mostly a humdrum, staid, and even a boring bunch of people. I should probably say 'erstwhile immediate folks', considering that we now have a separation of unfathomable depth between us and them. Anyway, the two of us have not seen this crazy impact too much on people we have been directly connected to hitherto.

But for Mojave and Bang, things are different. They are intimately connected with the streets, Bang more so than him, to be sure. But in their own ways, both have known so many highs and lows in terms of world contexts. They had been involved directly with people of extreme degrees of both good as well as evil. Of those people, a lot of them have fallen prey to what all is going on, as and when their evil side has been dominant within them, and that side has then succumbed to the Orenk attacks. Hence, this whole situation is a more personally painful matter for the two of them. They are seeing friends go down.

For me in particular, for most of my life I was not connected much to people at all, was always a loner. Not knowing good from evil, or truth from falsehood, or beauty from ugliness – had always tortured my soul. I grew up oscillating between the euphoria when instinct and inner sense showed me what's what and the anguish when that was missing, and I was clueless in terms of how to distinguish the instances that life threw my way, for each of the above cited fuzzily binary categories.

Anyway, enough moping about us now, let's move along. The fight is right in our faces. This is no time to get philosophical. With the enemy so clearly identified, the categories are no longer that fuzzy anyway. We can directly identify whatever is evil, false, and ugly, since it is not hidden any more.

But, at a level deeper than what this targeted state of alien colonization implies, I can't really say what exactly it is that is going on with the people of the earth now. There is the obvious and evident epidemic level increase of the manubrium bond induced loping gait and concomitant symptoms, and its correlation with those we know who have a stronger predilection towards evil, as defined from a human perspective. It gets metaphysical, beyond that. The bad ones have a thing for sulfur. Our mythologies have recognized that for ages now.

We finish the check-in and board our flight. I tell the team that per Randy's blade cuts we should expect to no longer show the lope, so everyone is relieved at least on that front.

I continue the rest of my chain of thought while in the air.

The newsfeeds we are getting reflect the dire countdown. Things are degenerating fast. On the streets, in the market places, business establishments, government situations, everywhere. Seems like just the other day that we had met with Detective Pat Murphy at his precinct, wonder how he is doing now. Today, it is unlikely that any public institution such as a police station is functioning normally. There has been drastic deterioration in a matter of days.

People are dropping like lemmings all around. No one is able to even keep track of the almost innumerable neurodegenerative diseases that are striking humankind at a dizzying rapid pace, bunch of new ones each day. People seem to be felled by a fast track version of Alzheimer's or some such thing, and then some of them crop right back up like zombies, but held now by the sword. The Orenk have worked out ways to hurt us where it really hurts, right in our protein interactions. They are piggybacking on existing diseases like rye pollen asthma, and deploying their phages on top.

The world has changed a lot in the past few generations. For the past half century or so or maybe even longer than that, there has been no major hegemony or empire that dominates. The USA has become a placeholder entity for that purpose, and the power play that goes on in Washington D.C. is routinely up for grabs by the usurper of the day, depending on which geo-political element around the world has muscle to flex for the moment. They just drive the lobbies, and the American machine executes as per their ephemeral demands. The chaos is maddening. The world has become a free for all.

In this crazy messed up situation, how can we fight an invasive, extra-terrestrial enemy?

Well, the baton is with me. I am The Conch.

So how do we fix up this whole mess now? First, one needs to understand the fabric before weaving cloth from it. What is the true essence of a human being? No hang on, let's step back. Even as The Conch, that is a bigger bite than I can chew.

So, do we Band-Aid it from the outside for now? That is probably the expedient thing to do. The deeper fix to human nature can be deferred for a later time.

The thing to do immediately is to find antidotes for the Orenk introduced ills in our biome. Some things have to be done quite rapidly, such as reviving the phytoplankton community in our water bodies. At the human scale, the Orenk have targeted our metabolic pathways and cellular system interactions. We need to come up with micro RNA solutions that need to be deployed in bulk across the globe, and quite rapidly at that. Corrective measures need to be applied to the air and water. We have to look into cloud seeding. The last leg of fixing up a person will be oligodendrocyte precursor cell programming to regain myelination.

While I muse thus, in parallel an instinct kicks in, and as a reflex I instantiate a conch measure as to what the most immediate threat is to our ecosystem.

Whoa, man! As we are flying thirty thousand feet above the ground, I get a Conch measure that all over the world it is shaping up to be doomsday time, missiles with nuclear warheads are in various stages of preparation and activation. Just like Memo had anticipated when he set up Bang with the shape-shifting power, the real ugly stuff is starting to happen now.

At a conscious level, I don't even know *how* I get these measures. Could it be fissile traces in the immediate atmosphere outside our aircraft that carry an electromagnetic signature that my brain is picking up, who knows? I have no idea. One thing I'm sure of is, that the measures that instantiate in my head, they all pertain to key Orenk doings. Bonar seems to have programmed it so.

The immediate task now for us will be to deactivate the warheads already in flight, then address the ones about to take flight, and finally defuse the remaining ones that are as of yet incubating.

Being The Conch, I assume command in Memo's absence. As soon as we disembark at JFK, I validate the media RSS feeds for corroboration, and damn it, I was right. No one else can figure it out yet, since based on what is on TV or other forms of media, there seem to be no hints yet, but I can read the hidden message. Soon enough it will get discovered by others or the news will be leaked, but that will be too late for any corrective action.

I instruct Bang and Mojave to head over to where the warhead is in flight, defuse it, and divert it into the sea, or in the worst case further up in the atmosphere.

Meanwhile, Montaña and I will continue over to the Beacon Headquarters, since we have to keep up the appearances of being Orenk stooges. Surely we will have to provide a status update soon enough.

Once we successfully reconvene, all four of us will go around the world and scramble up all the nuclear codes, so that at least none can go off till we figure out a more robust solution.

We step out of the arrivals terminal and take a cab to Idlewild Park. We need to work out a strategy, but quickly. The warhead is in flight already.

We get off at the park and walk over to a marshy patch of grass.

"So, is it time to fly out?" Mojave asks. He is itching to try out the power.

"Let's find a quieter spot, to minimize the chronology protection impact," I say. That is a hard thing to do in New York, even at Idlewild Park. We hardly have a minute or so between one bunch of passersby and another.

"Glad you are thinking straight, Conch," Memo joins us again, just at the right time.

"The first in-flight warhead has been shot out of Indonesia, and is on a trajectory towards somewhere in Burma," I tell them. No idea why this is happening, the countries in question have not even had any conflict in the past.

The world is getting overrun by Orenk infested people, there won't be much logic behind actions such as this, for us to decipher. We just have to intercept and defuse. Presumably, some of the military and/or scientific personnel involved have turned extreme lope, and those are the ones I'm receiving the measures for. I can't really explain how I know it; the initial setup inside my head was done by Bonar.

Officially, that is to say based on the various versions of the non-proliferation treaty, most countries are supposed to not even be in possession of nuclear weapons. What we are seeing in action is very different though. All kinds of bootleg stuff shows rampant, all across the world.

We are soldiers now though, our job is to just find the problem and solve it.

We come upon a grotto, from within which Bang and Mojave will take flight now.

"Fly safe," I tell them. "Memo will guide you along as you go."

"How do we do that? Where do we get the aerodynamic lift from?" Mojave asks.

"You know the Haka warrior dance?" Memo says. "Do it, and when you get it right, you'll get the necessary thrust and vertical acceleration."

They try, and Memo shakes his head sadly at their pathetic attempt.

"Let me show you the proper moves," he says.

They follow along, and momentarily they are airborne, taking off in a rapid zip. I hope that no one was able to see them.

"Head over to Beacon now, the two of you," Memo tells Montaña and me. "I will take care of this end."

We need a plan though. It takes me a moment, and it comes to mind right on cue. We will rebrand the intended subversion as an enhancement.

We will propose a feature set on top of the standard Beacon offering that caters to fantasy fulfillment. People can explore image changes, for themselves as also for those that arouse them to an extent already, and further arousal can be achieved by fantasy role play. For this, what we will suggest is for the Beacon Virtualization Infrastructure to have networks set up for moving virtual machines across data loci, all to be done without too much IT surgery. The virtual CPUs are already allocated to IP v6 addresses, and the server side systems are thus networked to frontend addresses, which are of course items of clothing, the Beacon Apparel. This virtualization is to be managed via 'Realized Orchestration'. These operations will also be run from the back office at Shahabad. I am formulating the sales pitch as we go.

To the Orenk stooges, we will pitch this as a means by which we will shoehorn the infection in. But, at an opportune moment, we will bail on that idea. Although there might still be merit and a business case for it as far as the intrinsic idea itself is concerned, minus the Orenk infection of course.

My job is to sell the rebranding and Montaña's job is to convince the Beacon bosses that this will not compromise their security. There are several holes in this plan of course, but we'll fix them over iterations.

It will take a while for Bang and Mojave to return from the South East Asian airspace, and in the meantime, Montaña and I should get enough traction on this plan for the Orenk to feel secure with regards to their hold on us.

Memo will meanwhile set up a laboratory for us in Death Valley, hidden underground below the dry bed of a Pleistocene lake, where we can work out things like oligodendrocyte precursor cell programming solutions to cure infected lopers, and whatever other technology solutions we need to come up with for this fight. We might not have the scientific background for it, but I can always pull together Conch blueprints and step by step instructions, and we can further tinker along based off of that, in the lab.

"How will we get all the materials and supplies we need? For any given experiment, we need to run a series of trial and error chemical reactions, and the supply list will not be trivial," I wonder out loud.

"For now, Mojave's got money, we'll set up a supply chain for these purposes once he returns," says Memo. "Going forward, for all of your personal needs you will gradually switch to tapping Visceral sources, so things like terrestrial money will not be a personal requirement beyond a point, for any of you. So we might as well use his existing stash for this good purpose, because for this particular requirement which is for the human population at large, it is best to work with local resources and I would rather not intervene Viscerally, unless it becomes the last resort. The less we tinker with the chronological balance for the overall population, the better it would be for our world."

We mull on that for a bit, and then Montaña and I head over to Manhattan, to the Beacon Headquarters. There, Montaña will lobby for a meeting with the board of executives where she will pitch that I have an idea that will be highly profitable for Beacon.

Her access card into the building does not work when she tries to swipe it. The people at the front desk are puzzled as to why, because the card diagnostics all return positive results. They just magnetize the strip again, and it works for her this time. I get a visitor card in the meantime.

She tries to introduce me there, as the guy who has done those Conch deals for Beacon in the past, intending to prove my mettle for this sales pitch. I feel like a butterfly whose track record as a caterpillar is being peddled.

I think I understand what is going on, as to why people are finding it hard to remember me, and why Montaña's card acted up as well. We are seeing the effects of chronology protection. Along further interactions as well, it proves to be hard indeed to cite my prior work, even though I have not explicitly exposed any aspects of what I gained from the Visceral trip. Just the way in which our body is fighting off the manubrium hold is in itself an exposure. Therefore, we are automatically distanced from fellow humans, so much so that they cannot even connect with my past work. We barely manage to make the connection, just about enough to secure an interview with the executive board. James Carter is the Chief Information Officer and Kuo Huang is the Chief Security Officer. The front office tells us that we will be informed when the two of them will have an open slot for our appointment.

I realize that chronology protection will hit each of us more and more as we go. Montaña will not be able to go back to her day job as Emmy. By the time this war is over, her records will mysteriously be blocked or submerged or whatever it is that is to happen, somewhat similar to how all traces of Bonar got wiped out, way back when. My post doc days are over as well. Our old lives are rapidly fading away behind us, in our wake.

No time for wallowing in commiseration, we need to just keep on keeping on. We're at war.

James Carter and Kuo Huang have a custom of taking their families for a Lake Ontario winter fishing holiday in Upstate New York. Trout and walleye is what they fish for, at this time of the year. They agree to give us a breakfast audience there at their holiday destination. These executives work round the clock and calendar, I'm impressed.

So Montaña and I rent a car and start out for Mexico, New York.

She's driving. "All set, partner?" I ask rhetorically. "Are we ready to dismantle and undo Bonar's legacy of intrusion prevention at Beacon?"

It is nice now that we both are respectively paired romantically to other people we have finally arrived at a platonic equilibrium.

"Are we really going to do that, what if we end up having to follow it through all the way to the end, and destroy Beacon in the bargain?" she asks.

"No we're not," I reassure her. "This thing is not going to last too long. We just need to keep up appearances at least up to the point where we have the advantage, when our cover is blown."

On Highway 81 North, there is a lane stack from Scranton to Binghamton where the express lanes are on the upper tier. Montaña has a thing for driving standard, stick shift, and all that, rather than depending on the vector controls. Which is all fine and dandy until a hitch happens, like what almost does take place with us right now.

We both are admiring some wind turbines that are set up in some of the hilly terrain of Upstate New York that we are passing through, and I mention that they remind me of an Ennyk song called *Windmills and Terrapins*, and Montaña turns her head towards me to give me a quizzical look. In the process, we struggle to merge into the required lane. We nearly miss the entrance ramp for the upper tier express lanes but barely make it.

We reach Mexico, NY late in the evening and sleep in early, so that we can be fresh and ready for the morning.

The next day we have a nice breakfast meeting with the Beacon executives. Their fishing trip into the lake will start the next day. They are smart boys. The way they talk about network corralling is reminiscent of cowboy speak of the Wild West in the days of yore. We share the high level of our idea with them, and discuss some further platitudes about how to harvest the edge regions of the out-of-band portion of the Beacon network for some pilot attempts, and then head back.

Memo speaks to us over the Bluetooth car phone as we are driving towards New York City. "I got Mojave and Bang to execute a manual override code on the warhead," he says, "and we also gave a vertical lift to the ballistic device so that the explosion will occur high enough in the atmosphere to reduce the effect on the surface biome to a minimum, and also even though the explosion will take place unfortunately, we prevented the chain reaction so it won't be too bad."

Well, that's a relief, overall.

When we reach New York City, Memo has made sure that Bang and Mojave are already there, waiting for us right where we stop for a late lunch.

"Hey there, high fliers," Montaña hollers at them. They smile wanly, looking utterly exhausted. Notwithstanding the Visceral boosts that we receive via Memo, looks like this superhero stuff is going to be tiring.

"How was it?" I ask eagerly, nonetheless.

"Well, we have to watch out for a lot of stuff when we're up there, quite aside from the birds and the man-made air traffic" Bang replies, "the horse latitudes, for example. Without Memo's protection, it's like we'd be raked over coals."

"Don't forget the doldrums either, those can get real nasty too," Mojave says.

"Was it fun though?" I ask.

"Well, duh, yeah!" he grins, looking at me like as though I'm a laboratory specimen. Of course it was fun.

Kaboom

Well, there you have it, we are officially superheroes now. Bang and Mojave have flown across the troposphere on a hero mission. My Conch ability doesn't really trigger this sense of having become a superhero, since it is something that just goes on under wraps. This flying thing though, it is textbook hero material, or rather, comic book material to be precise.

It is time to celebrate a little bit. Not that we can relax too much, the battle is still on, but we should definitely relish the victories along the way.

We head over to Coney Island to unwind. It is winter, not many people are near the beach. We find it nice and peaceful, and spend a good few hours there. We then sleep early, since the next few days are going to be particularly hectic.

I end up having to stay local, to maintain the front for the cartel goons. Bang, Montaña, and Mojave fly around the world, shape-shifting into lookalikes of military and scientific personnel of various countries, and neutralizing their nuclear arsenals. Memo even provides them with the features for copying biometric signatures, like fingerprints and eyeball scans. They're having fun.

I roam the streets of New York, taking in the sights and keeping the goons updated, while waiting for the team to return. During this time, my head gets filled with a deluge of Conch measures that keep instantiating and piling up, and for which I have no outlets. I need to siphon them off to the team for execution, or else I'll go crazy.

Then in a few days, the team returns.

"All missions accomplished?" I ask. Mojave nods and I breathe a sigh of relief. Now it is time for the next steps.

"I wouldn't pop the champagne yet though," Montaña reins it in a bit. "We scrambled their nuclear codes, and deferred their nefarious plans for now. But it is only a short reprieve. Their machineries are whirring along on recovery paths."

Fair enough, but I'm happy for the moment. As long as the nuclear winter is not looking like it's slotted for this week some time, I have the margin to plan out the extended defense, and I can work with that. Now we need to shift focus to healing the biome a bit, I believe.

Once we return to California, I intend to head over to our cell programming lab in Death Valley to work out practical details on some ideas that have fermented in my head the past few days. Mojave offers to show me around when we get there. That area is his territory after all.

"Thanks bud," I tell him. "I know those are your digs there, but we have to divide and conquer. There is a heck of a lot we have to do all over the world, and real quick, at that. There will be more pressing engagements for you to run with, things like what you were doing the past few days, in one form or the other basically."

We're nearly done here in New York, just need to provide a final status update to some local Orenk stooges and then we can head back to the West Coast.

One of the things that had come to my mind while I was mucking around town waiting for the gang, is a far out political concept. I might as well broach the subject while we wait for directions from the local cartel thugs.

"Hey fellas, we need a changing of the guards on the world leadership front. Let's ride on FTL," I tell the team. "I'm not talking about 'Faster than Light', like what Bonar was referring to, the acronym here stands for 'Follow the Leader'."

"What are you talking about, buddy?" Mojave asks.

I explain the details, as best as I understand them. I do believe the concept holds much promise.

FTL is a social media experiment that has led to the designation of a World Leader every year. It is by intent and definition a theoretical role. Li Chin, a political science student from The University of Singapore came up with the idea that every world citizen can run for this theoretical office. From each country, a leading individual arises as their country's proposed candidate for this role, the one who obtains the most endorsements in this social media game, within the said country.

From out of all the designated candidates from all the countries, one is then selected as the World Leader, based on the same logic now played out at a world level, the constraint being that no one can vote for their own country's candidate. This selected person is now designated as the World Leader for the year and gets to provide theoretical inputs pertaining to world affairs, to the governing bodies of any given country. Of course, so far most of the chosen candidates have mainly basked in the fifteen minutes of fame thus obtained and haven't really had enough real power to be able to be politically effective. Some have provided good insights for long term policies, and have been duly acknowledged. I believe the time has come to bestow more teeth to this role.

"The FTL world leaders to date have shown a good track record in terms of how they are regarded," I say. "They have influenced people's behavior well and are properly influenced by it, in turn. They reflect the pulse of humankind. So let's equip them with the necessary power and authority now. We will have to strategically influence various lobbies and policy structures worldwide, for this to come into effect."

"To fight enemies like the Orenk, we will need centralized world leadership. I see your point," Mojave agrees.

"We will have to covertly influence events in such a manner that this World Leader becomes a decision maker," Montaña chips in. "Agencies such as the FDA and the EPA will only comply when they have no other recourse. The reining in of all such recalcitrant entities has to be done in conjunction with world level centralization."

It is a good concept to keep refining in the background, while we continue to deal with tactical goals in the immediate term.

Here is what is going on with the world right now. People are falling prey to all kinds of wrong passions. It starts like this: there are a lot of rather bad people in the world, and among them many are highly passionate about something or the other. Of the remaining humans, i.e. those who are by and large fairly good, a lot of them feel the lack of some form of passion, and end up falling under the spell of someone else's some stupid passion or the other. Once they become invested in it, their ego forces them to internalize and legitimize that particular perspective, and gradually they turn bad themselves, even if that had not been their intention.

For example, they might see themselves as champions of a threatened way of life even if the threat is entirely fictitious, just because someone else invented the threat out of their hat but did so passionately. Such people then fall prey to the manipulations of unscrupulous tyrants. Those who are content enough with their natural and innate extent of passion, become an increasingly dwindling minority.

Now, the tyrants have been superseded by predatory and invasive aliens, but the same principle continues to apply. The Orenk are targeting vulnerable pockets of humans based on this strategy.

A common form of bad passion is hatred of some other category of humans. It gives some kind of an atavistic pleasure to a lot of people and we see patterns of aggregation of such people all through the annals of history. This is what we have to fight first, before we can form a front against alien invaders. For this, the FTL model might be a good idea to pursue further.

So yes, we'll work on this FTL angle in the long run, but for now we have to deal with the battles of the day.

"Anyway, these are all rough cut ramblings in the head, for the future." I wrap up this topic for now. "The time will come for these things, but for now we have to fight at tactical levels. Let's get on with the show."

The East Coast Orenk stooges finally give us an audience. We knock off the charade with them and step out of there, glad to have that load off our chest.

Now, we fly back to L.A., this time all four of us. I am the clumsiest with the Haka dance, and it gets even harder since they all roast me mercilessly at my tragic attempts, but ultimately I manage to work the moves and we take off. The American airspace is crowded. The views and sceneries are fabulous though, and I find it hard to keep up with the rest. They've done it a few times already and it's almost become routine for them, but I want to relish my first flight.

We reach L.A. Mojave's apartment continues to be our base.

One day, I get an urgent measure in my head, that there is some high risk activity shaping up that will affect the entire population of L.A., and the signs of it point to Pauline, one of our old banes.

Montaña and Mojave are on critical missions in the Central European and West Asian regions at this time.

Bang has enough inside knowledge to be able to get to the target, but she will need backup and the only remaining option is me. I have no fighting background though, so she has to teach me before I can be of use.

First, she equips me with a New Generation Colt .45, then takes me to a firing range and shows me basic safety techniques and how to shoot reasonably straight and be able to handle the recoil.

"So where is Pauline?" Bang asks.

"Somewhere in the Platinum Triangle, either Beverly Hills or Bel Air," I respond. I don't understand how I get the knowledge about these things, but so far it is proving to be quite accurate, this query response mechanism. I am getting used to being an instrument for a larger cause.

Momentarily, I get the proper zoom level and the accurate detailed location.

We drive over to the address my head is leading us to, and Bang uses her skeleton key skills to let us in. We can hear Pauline in the basement, swearing loudly.

"Why don't you just kill me?" A young girl's whimpering voice responds to the swearing.

"I have to go do something now, but I will come back to finish this job too, yes," Pauline seems to be replying to the girl.

We hear the sound of someone running up the stairs, and hide in a room to the side. It is Pauline. Once she leaves, we go downstairs, and find the girl who is tied up and seems to have been brutally tortured. There are all kinds of ghastly tools in here; chain saws, prods, bridles, thumbscrews, ropes, and chairs. I shudder. The girl is severely maimed, so we release her and radio Memo to come by and heal her. The girl is too distraught, and insists that Bang stay.

"You go and stop Pauline. I'll take a cab and join you once Memo shows up, text me the address when you get a chance," Bang tells me.

The guideline for us, per Memo, is to make judicious use of our Haka powered flight ability, and whenever possible adopt the ways of the world, such as cab rides. This way, we can hold on to our terrestrial imprints for longer. At the end of the day though, we will all have to convert over to Visceral form and become ghosts as far as the earth is concerned, but might as well delay the inevitable to the extent that we can.

I head out on the chase.

Pauline is heading towards Owens Lake.

As I catch up with her there, she is just about to board a helicopter. My readings indicate that she intends to dump some chemicals into the lake, such that the Second Aqueduct and other flow lines that provide water from the lake to L.A. will transmit some form of damage to the city's population. I'm caught off guard. So far, I was aware of the Orenk spores hitting us only via the nervous system, as is the case with the manubrium bond. Now, this thing that Pauline it trying to do seems to indicate that they have other means of infecting us too, via the circulatory, digestive, and other systems as well possibly. We'll need to dig deeper into that. But the first thing to do is to stop Pauline. She sees me as I approach, and starts firing at me right away.

As of now, Montaña is the only one among us with the skill of deflecting bullets, but she is not here right now. So, I do run the risk of getting seriously maybe even fatally injured in this battle, if I try to give Pauline a fighting chance. If that happens, then I'll depend totally on Memo to revive me. Sure, he would be able to do that, but that would be a heck of a lot of overhead I'd be imposing on him, it would be best to not get hit at all.

I don't have the reflexes and the skills to engage in direct gunfight, so I'm scared and nervous. But still, it is the task on hand, so I raise the colt and take aim. I do have the advantage that Pauline has multiple distractions and tasks she needs to execute. She is about to board the chopper, so it is now or never.

In this extenuating circumstance, I reluctantly conclude that I am licensed to kill her. I take the shot as soon as I have line of sight, and kill Pauline.

Such is our role, as defenders of the human race and the earth. It comes at gut wrenching cost. Back at UCSC, I could have never imagined that I would be taking a human life one day. This thing is taking its toll on me.

On the whole, mine is the heavy task of judging who has turned extreme lope and become an irredeemable e-loper, since I am the Conch, for better or for worse. When we round up miscreants, this is the decision tree we will face: if Memo finds it feasible to gather them into a Shifter trip and purge their infection thereby, then that is an okay outcome, we will hand them over to Memo. Alternately, if we are able to find some antidote here itself, and push the point of no return further back, that is good too. If time does not permit either of these methods, then the crew will be licensed to kill the identified e-lopers, considering that the survival of the entire carbon based biome is at stake.

Even from battlegrounds where they currently are at, whenever they are at crossroads, Montaña and Mojave call me before taking a life.

We are starting to evolve a cadre structure.

Bang has made it here in the meantime. She walks over to me, sees my grim face, and understands what has happened, and hugs me tight. Memo will clean up the mess as usual. There's the body to be dealt with, and the disposal of the chemicals in the chopper.

"I'll haul the stuff from the chopper over to our lab in Death Valley, we can analyze it later," Memo says.

Bang and I head back to Mojave's place.

I sense that the Orenk are gradually getting to recognize us as the prime threat even though they wouldn't know the source of our powers, and they will direct their prime arsenal specifically at us four. The rest of mankind will just feel the ripples, but won't really know what's going on at our level.

Days go by.

Somewhere along this timeframe, we enter the New Year. For a while now, I have spent most of my time in the lab, coming back only to test out my potions on guinea pig lopers, so to speak.

"I think I have some good news," I finally announce.

"What is it?" Bang asks.

"I believe I have worked out a successfully proven antidote to the xiphoid hold," I say. "It is a means by which the infected human regains original state of myelination and is rid of the evil touch. We have to catch some test cases now and verify."

"Okay, let me step out and grab one for you," she says and vanishes. In a short while, she returns with a trussed up e-loper who is frothing at the mouth, a nasty piece of work.

We perform systematic homeostasis, insulation, restructuring, and gluing of breakages in the impacted neurons by means of precursor cell programming on his central nervous system, to correct the effect of the xiphoid hold on him and destroy pathogens. It seems to work, as far as I can tell.

Now we know how to cure all and any of the infected ones. The point of no return has been effectively erased for all but the most inveterate ones. We can now fight with no cause for qualms of conscience at having to take lives that could have been salvaged, to the most part.

Then, one day, Randy and Wanda show up, along with Carlos. My Conch reading confirms that they have traced Pauline's elimination to us. The cover is fully blown now.

"You're on the hook if any of them escapes," Carlos screams at Randy.

They try to shoot us down, but Montaña deflects their bullets. Our guns are out now. They are shocked at this, and retreat to revise their strategy.

Now *we* chase.

As The Conch, I hold the scales of justice. I draft out the license to kill these three, since my Conch reading tells me they are sold to their cause and even the antidote will not fix them. It is not about the biochemical point of no return of the infection at all, their core personalities have gone dark basically. We have no choice with them.

"My reading is that they're headed for Dana Point," I tell the crew. We head out in Mojave's ride, the one about which he just can't stop talking about, he goes on and on about the gears and clutches, and combinations thereof. The girls are appreciative of the car and engage meaningfully in the conversation with him, while I focus on the chase.

We find our targets on the road and shoot at them, driving them off the Pacific Coast Highway near Newport Beach. We are driving like as though we're in Toon Town, performing crazy acrobatics aided by Memo, just to avoid hitting other cars and pedestrians.

Those goons on the other hand have no such qualms and unfortunately, they cause a lot of damage, which hopefully Memo is able to fix and clean up.

"Ah, there's The Crab Cooker," says Mojave. "I love the food there."

Well, that's great, but the traffic around it is horrendous to say the least, especially in the context of this car chase.

Randy and Co are heading to Balboa Pier. By the time we catch up with them there, they are about to take off in a custom built dive boat, out into the relatively chilly January waters of the Pacific Ocean.

Their boat is so fancy that it triggers a sharp exclamation of approval from Mojave. Memo rapidly upgrades Mojave's car, to make it amphibious. We hit the waters and continue the chase.

The dive boat reaches Santa Catalina Island where they try to dock and try to shoot at us hoping for better luck this time. Once again, when that doesn't work for them, they back out of the dock and head further out into the waters. We leave them no room for slack, and gradually catch up with them, just as they're about to reach Santa Rosa Island.

At Skunk Point, it looks like they intend to moor their boat. Presumably they've scoped out the place, and believe that it will be a vantage point for them.

"Let's cut to the chase," says Bang. She looks around and the place is deserted except for us and them. She then invokes her elemental power, the one she had asked Bonar for while aboard the klystron, and as if by magic she is on a surfboard with a swell of waves propelling her towards the goons' boat, just as they are about to moor. "Montaña, do the usual if you could, please," she shouts.

There is a flurry of bullets being shot at Bang, of course. Montaña gets on the job and duly deflects them all.

Our boat is close enough now, we have line of sight. Joe and Montaña knock off Randy and Wanda respectively.

Carlos is left, he is screaming with rage.

"Montaña, can you get his gun?" Bang shouts. "I want him to go down by his own bullet." She must have her reasons. There is much history between the two of them.

Montaña obliges, and transfers Carlos's gun to me.

Meanwhile, Bang grabs Carlos by the collar, and pounds him senseless. Then, having settled her accounts and shed her demons, she calmly surfs her way back to our boat.

I have the gun with me, so I guess I'm the one who has drawn his number. One shot, and the deed is done.

"Leave the gun, take the cannoli," Bang says to me.

I don't quite follow. "Don't worry about it," she says, noticing my quizzical look. "It's a tip of the hat at an old classic. Let's go home."

Memo cleans the slate on the island, and we head back to Joe's pad.

Thereafter, multiple encounters occur, with other Orenk minions of smaller orders. We just truss them up and fix them using antidotes, and then release them.

Next, I take inventory of various consumer and healthcare products which have been targets of Orenk subversion, and identify the associated corporate entities. We have to clean up their act as well.

"Team, it will get busy now," I say. I feel proud of the steely resolve in their faces, in response to my statement.

"There is much to do, a long road ahead of us," I continue.

"Sure, we'll git 'er done, all of it," Mojave says. "First, we need a collective name, a tag by which people will know of us."

"People won't know of us, remember chronology protection?" I remind him.

"That's okay. Let's have a name, even if it is just for us. We are The Spectral League," Montaña responds. "I'm thinking of the spectral theorem in Fourier analysis, and the resolution of the identity. At the same time, we might as well come to terms with the fact that gradually we will shed our corporeal presence here trading it in for Visceral identities, and eventually we'll also turn into ghosts here, and join Memo in the league of specters on earth. Hence, we are the spectral league."

"Fine, that's who we are," I agree. "So let's get on with it. We have to clean up shop for each of the infected enterprises. Let's start with Chariot." I'm looking at Mojave in particular, since he still works there.

"The pillow manufacturing is in Guatemala," he says. "So we will make a trip there to kick off this cleanup. Tell us what to do."

"We will have to put in a lot of grunt work, buddy," I say. "When we go on site, we will have to become shape-shifter lookalikes of key personnel in the shop floor areas of these enterprises, and step by step eliminate the infection process in the production line. The details of the plan will evolve as we go."

"That sounds like fun," says Montaña.

"Also, the same sort of effort will be required, to influence the reworking of corporate policies and procedures as well at the headquarters, to prevent further breaches in the future," I add.

"That does *not* sound like fun," Mojave grimaces.

All in all of course, they're game. I continue to work out mission details from base, and they go do the magic on location. Some days go by.

From the Death Valley lab, we also figure out ways to correct for the Orenk impact across the biome, how to apply cleaning chemicals to the water tables all over the world, how to use cloud seeding methods, phytoplankton revival in the natural water bodies, and multiply such measures.

I take stock around mid-March. Our efforts seem to have taken effect to a large extent, as best as we can make out. The number of people exhibiting the behavior related to a held xiphoid is trending down now. As far as my Conch readings indicate, and as borne out by our actual observations as well, we seem to have pushed the Orenk back, even if we have not yet fully cleansed the world of this infection.

"All these cleaning up activities," Mojave mutters, "we're basically doing janitorial work. I had thought being superheroes would be exciting."

"Hey Mojave, here's a cool idea. Why don't you go take another dunk?" Montaña teases him. "See if Daithi still has the lope?"

"No thanks, I'll pass," says a visibly embarrassed Mojave.

"The Orenk themselves though, have we really beaten them? Have they fully retreated from our Solar System?" he further wonders.

"They're down, but I don't think they're out," Bang exhales heavily. "This thing is going to be really long drawn …"

"Yes, something doesn't add up about the whole matter," Montaña agrees with her. "Over the course of the fight with Carlos, Randy, and Wanda, I was finding it incrementally more difficult to deflect their bullets. It felt as though they were calling on counteracting powers. That definitely has to be something bigger than the Orenk stooge deal."

They might be on to something, let me execute a Conch measure.

This is proving to be a tough one for the Conch. Are there more hidden powers on the enemy side than what we've come to grips with so far? The Conch outtake is to check with Memo, hand over the game to the bigger gun.

"I will do a deep check," he says. He freezes for a moment, and then frees up and executes an indescribably awe inspiring action. We have never seen him like this before. From our vantage point, what we see now is the specter of a dog experiencing a divine moment. His shape, look, and feel is reminiscent of the sensory blasts which we underwent on the Klystron, during our wormhole traversal.

After a while, he is back.

"I bring grim tidings," says Memo. "Indeed, there are higher powers at play. The Orenk have only temporarily retreated. They, or more likely some other entities who control them, have access to The Dark Book."

"What is that?" I ask.

"All along the annals of various Visceral cultures there have been various suppressed hints of its existence," Memo says heavily. "But they have never been strong references, just furtive hints. Unlike its counterpart the Glorious Book of Light, about which there has always been legend and lore galore, even prior to its rediscovery by the Nomads in the Early-Chilled Era."

Memo does the spectral equivalent of taking a deep breath, and continues, "I now have the misfortune of having discovered that The Dark Book does exist. Evil beings in the thrall of the *Others* invoke its power, to fight those who are blessed by *Them*."

We have enough Visceral awareness by now, to know as to why The Greater Beings are to be only indirectly referenced. This is big, what Memo has found out! We will now need even stronger booster juices to be able to tackle this matter. But can we, even?

"This is like the Battle of Evermore," says Mojave, slowly clenching his palms into fists and then releasing them. "It's not just the Orenk, and it's not just what we are going through now. This has always been a much bigger cosmic game. All along our history, I'm sure humans have been players on occasion and pawns at times. The food chain is a never ending thing."

Something does ring true in what he says. Maybe we might just go back in time once in a way if the Shifter so allows, to learn some lessons on how to better deal with the future.

"Think back to what all Bonar had told you at the wishing well on the Klystron," Memo muses. "This whole arrangement of you having acquired Visceral superpowers, it comes with cosmic strings attached. Yes we have pushed the Orenk back for a bit, but the catch is that the bigger fish are biting now. Victory always comes with a price. In this case, what that translates to is that our world gets embroiled in a bigger war."

We are silent for a while.

"What all can we expect now?" asks Bang.

"You know, what we've dealt with so far was the easy bit," says Memo. He smiles, seeing that we all look startled. "The Orenk are our contemporaries, they are of our proper time and are comparable to us in terms of level of advancement. Maybe they have a bit of a technological edge over us, is the most that can be said for them. In contrast, the help we received from Bonar came from more than six billion years out in the future, and is therefore so very advanced, that even with just the slightest of help we managed to push the Orenk back."

We see his point.

"That said," Memo continues, "the constraint with any Visceral help we receive, is that which is imposed by chronology protection. We cannot breach the forbidden boundaries of the Cauchy Horizon. The grim aspect of what we will now have to prepare ourselves to deal with is that the forces of The Dark Book that come from the far future will have no such qualms or compunctions. They will not hesitate to create rifts in time."

"You're kidding us," I protest. "How is it that something that is impossible for A can be possible for B?"

"Those are the realms of evil which I myself do not have much comprehension of," Memo shares his sense of forlornness in a low voice.

"Be that as it may," Memo says further, mustering up resolve, "we will have to figure it out as we go. Keep up the good fight. The xiphoid hold will keep resurfacing, so don't let the guard down on that front. Aside from that, there will be many other signature elements of the enemy that we will have to watch out for. We will have to look deeper into what goes by the name of the Dark Web on the Earth - blocked and hidden IP addresses, crypto-currency, money that cannot be tracked, and all that. There will be so much more grunt work now."

Mojave groans.

"You are the ace team, you'll handle it just fine," Memo says encouragingly.

"We're ready, bring it on," I say.

"For sure, just hang on to your hats," Memo smiles. "Enjoy the spring now, look out for the summer blooms as they sprout, and continue to keep the world safe."

The girls smile. I'm exhausted, but manage a weak grin. Mojave shakes off his dour mood as well, and joins in for the group laugh.

We all sit back, and the sun goes down over the ocean.

About Som Nandivada

Som Nandivada is an IT Solutions Architect and an amateur musician (blues / classic rock: lyricist / drummer). He holds a Master's Degree in Mathematics, plus Graduate Credits in Physics and Space Studies. With this background, he is well positioned to explore the wonderful and fantastic possibilities that the domain of Science Fiction has to offer.

Social Media Links

Website: www.trihalya.com

Facebook: www.facebook.com/razorstropper

Twitter: https://twitter.com/somnandivada @somnandivada

Blog: https://trihalya.blogspot.ca/

Acknowledgements

To Conatus

If you enjoyed this story, check out these other Solstice Publishing books by Som Nandivida:

State/Craft Vision of the Seeker

The Super-Murals, Greater Entities from the beyond...

Eons from now, they are defeated and exiled by their nemesis, the Extra-Murals. As a part of the fallout, the Universe loses its advanced technological abilities.

Billions of years further along - The Book of Light, a manifesto put forth by the Super-Murals, is found. This Book was the one hope to revitalize a forgotten way of life.

Much later, as the Universe gets even colder and sentient life has evolved further, a being named Digger has a Vision.

Digger sees impending doom for trillions of lives, and the collapse of a revived Empire. But, there is a way out! A farm girl named Vega is to become queen. Only she can lead the battle against the nefarious Extra-Murals who threaten the existence of all that we know. The execution of the plan towards this vision also brings forth the return of the Nomads, creators of the Visceral Empire, quasi-immortal representatives of The Super-Murals. Felix, a man displaced in time, and forced to go down a path he never chose, is given the ability to use his mind for entrancement and control. Felix is the bridge to show Vega that she is meant to be queen.

They are guided by Arch-Pivot Nambu, an advanced

animal/machine composite sentient, also accompanied by Pinch, an inter-galactic bounty hunter.

Vega and Digger along with this unlikely team, set out to battle evil and to save life across the Universe.

Together, they defend our existence.

https://bookgoodies.com/a/B01M0IXI1U

www.ingramcontent.com/pod-product-compliance
Lightning Source LLC
Chambersburg PA
CBHW051645260626
47170CB00004B/1351